KU-688-141

TO LOVE AGAIN

After a disastrous romance in her youth, Juliet Radley has given up hope of marriage and become reconciled to a quiet life as Amy Gibson's governess. However, despite her expectations, she grows attached to Captain Richard Gibson, her employer's cousin — the only house guest to treat her with consideration. But a new arrival threatens her happiness: the rakish Hugh Faversham is the one man in the world who can expose her darkest secret . . .

Books by Jasmina Svenne
in the Linford Romance Library:

AGAINST ALL ODDS
THE RECLUSE OF
LONGWOOD PRIORY
MOONLIGHT AND SHADOW

JASMINA SVENNE

TO LOVE AGAIN

Complete and Unabridged

LINFORD
Leicester

First published in Great Britain in 2009

First Linford Edition
published 2009

Copyright © 2009 by Jasmina Svenne
All rights reserved

British Library CIP Data

Svenne, Jasmina M.
 To love again.- -(Linford romance library)
 1. Governesses- -Fiction.
 2. Love stories.
 3. Large type books.
 I. Title II. Series
 823.9′2–dc22

 ISBN 978–1–84782–907–8

WEST
DUNBARTONSHIRE
LIBRARIES

PRICE
£8·99

SUPPLIER
U

LOCATION
DP

CLASS
A F

INVOICE DATE

ACCESSION NUMBER
020298865

Published by
F. A. Thorpe (Publishing)
Anstey, Leicestershire
Set by Words & Graphics Ltd.
Anstey, Leicestershire
Printed and bound in Great Britain by
T. J. International Ltd., Padstow, Cornwall

This book is printed on acid-free paper

1

'Oh, Miss Radley, do come and look. You're missing all the fun.' Juliet looked up with a smile at her younger pupil. The slim twelve-year-old was perched sideways on the window seat, her forehead pressed to the glass to get the best view of the half-moon of gravel in front of the house. But despite the temptation that was held out to her, Juliet remained seated, her needle flashing as it inched its way round the vast circumference of the pink silk petticoat she was mending.

'Be careful. If anyone sees you there, we'll both be in trouble,' she replied.

Amy shook her head like a restive pony. As always, there was a loose strand of dark hair on her forehead, falling into her hazel eyes.

'They never look any higher than the first floor windows,' she replied. 'Do

1

come and see. Mrs Tibbs is wearing the most extraordinary hat.'

Juliet laid aside her sewing. Amy's enthusiasm was infectious and she was curious about the houseguests, though she had met some of them before. She placed herself behind her pupil and instinctively tucked the wayward lock behind Amy's ear. The girl glanced up with an amused smile, but as she tilted her head towards the drive, the same strand of hair fell across her face.

Juliet followed her gaze. She had missed most of the 'fun' as the ladies had already been disgorged from the coach and were disappearing from sight beneath the portico. But she watched with Amy as the coachman turned his vehicle and retraced his steps along the drive. Hidden behind the trees, a narrower path led to the stable-block.

There the horses would be unhitched and the trunks, bandboxes and other paraphernalia removed and conveyed up the backstairs to appear, as if by magic, in the bedrooms of the guests.

'How many is that then?' Juliet asked.

'There's Mrs Tibbs and the three Misses Tibbs, the two Mr Collins, Colonel and Mrs Halliday with their son and daughter, and Mr Parry all on his own,' Amy counted them off. 'Four, six, ten — eleven in all.'

'Well, there's nothing wrong with your arithmetic, or your memory,' Juliet remarked, returning to her sewing. 'Are any more expected?'

Amy remained seated by the window, though she turned inwards. Her white muslin gown looked crumpled, her cap was askew and a long, white-stockinged leg, dangling from beneath her petticoats, tapped against the wall.

'I can't think of anyone except Papa's cousin.' She tried the name out loud. 'Captain Richard Gibson.' Her gown rustled as she sat forward. 'I wish I could remember him better. Selina says he used to play with us when we were little, before he was sent to America.'

What with one thing and another, Juliet had heard a good deal about

Captain Gibson over the last weeks. For most of Amy's short life, Britain had been at war with the American rebels and their French and Spanish allies. Whenever a victory of any consequence occurred, Mr Gibson always arranged a bonfire and a feast for his neighbours and tenants.

A letter from his cousin would send him scurrying for the best maps he owned and, lacking a son to take an interest in such things, he had pointed out the locations of battlefields and sieges to his younger daughter.

As a result Amy now knew not only the whereabouts of New York, Philadelphia and Quebec, but also more obscure places like Germantown and Monmouth Courthouse. She had absorbed all the exciting tales and asked many questions that her father, as a civilian, was unable to answer. It was a pity, Juliet mused, that Amy had not been born a boy, to give her some scope for her boundless energy and curiosity.

Once Amy had exhausted the subject

of Captain Gibson, she moved on to other topics. Juliet let her chatter. Having been the Gibsons' governess for the past three years, she knew there was no hope of coaxing Amy into any extraordinary feats of scholarship on this day of all days and so had granted her an unofficial holiday, provided Mamma and Papa never found out.

It was small wonder Amy was excited. For the best part of the winter and spring, the house had been all but deserted, save for Amy, her governess and a reduced staff of servants. Mrs Gibson had deemed that her other daughter, Selina, was old enough to make her first entrance into polite society, despite being only fifteen, and so the rest of the family had spent the season in London.

Juliet had done her best to entertain Amy, but it was obvious she often missed her sister, no matter how much they bickered when they were together. They had never been separated before and, despite good intentions, neither was a diligent correspondent. Selina, kept busy day after day, never found time to write to Amy, after her first two or three laborious tussles with the mysteries of English spelling, found she had nothing more to say about being stranded in the Herefordshire country-side in the depths of winter.

Then at last a letter had arrived announcing the imminent return of the Gibsons to Winfield Hall, to be closely followed by a houseful of guests.

'Were you ever in love, Miss Radley?'

The question took Juliet by surprise, not having followed the train of Amy's monologue attentively enough.

'I hardly think that is any of your business,' she replied, suppressing a twinge of memory.

'Why not? You're not so very much older than me.'

Suddenly Juliet was overwhelmed by the urge to laugh. With difficulty she retained her cool expression.

'I am a full sixteen years older than you and your parents employ me to teach you, not to make you my confidante. So if you don't settle down, I'll set you some French verbs to learn.'

But Amy had clearly ignored all but the first part of her reply.

'Are you really twenty-eight?' she asked. 'That's only eight years younger than Mamma.'

Amy had always been good with numbers, even at quite a young age. But when Juliet first arrived at Winfield Hall, she had discovered Amy's reading and writing lagged woefully behind her active mind, as she had a vivid imagination and loved to have stories read aloud to her. From what Selina and Amy had told her, they had run rings around their previous governess and Amy's imagination in particular had been put to use in inventing new forms of rebellion.

'You don't look old,' Amy added when there was no reply.

'Thank you.'

Juliet glanced involuntarily towards the window in which she could see a faint image of herself. Perhaps it was ner round cheeks that gave her a youthful look, or the fact she had never used cosmetics and so had escaped their corrosive effects. Her hair too was dressed in a simple knot, rather than in the higher, more extravagant style favoured by fashionable ladies.

But Amy was not done yet.

'If you're twenty-eight, why aren't you married yet?'

Juliet suppressed a wince. There were sometimes whole days now when she did not think about her past and then something trivial would serve to remind her. She had no intention of telling Amy the truth, however.

'Nobody asked me,' she replied.

'Why not?'

'Because I am too poor and too plain. And now, if you have no objections, I want to see if Selina's headache is any better.'

Juliet swept across the room, closing the door behind her. It was a risk leaving Amy alone while she was in this mood. Mischief sometimes seemed to be in her blood. But she could not stay in that room a second longer.

For a moment she paused in the windowless corridor, which was illuminated only by an open door at its far end leading to the back stairs.

Juliet tapped at the next door and as she entered, she distinctly heard the scuffle of paper being concealed in a pocket or perhaps simply beneath the spreading skirts of the girl's lavender blue gown.

Selina too had been gazing out of the small window under the sloping ceiling, but her pose suggested listlessness. Like her sister, she was dark-haired, though hers had been dressed in a fashionable style, partly piled up, partly tumbling in apparently artless ringlets. Her face looked very youthful beneath this sophisticated coiffure. In the last year, she had grown so rapidly, it had been hard work making sure her petticoats were long enough to conceal her ankles, but her figure had not yet filled out.

'Any better?' Juliet asked, mustering

a cheerful smile.

'A little. I think I'll be able to go down to dinner,' Selina replied, but she sighed and there was a look of longing in her eyes.

Juliet felt a twitch of alarm. Selina had always been quieter than her sister, but she had not been herself since her return from London. She looked pale, ate little, gazed out of windows, complained of sleeping badly and seemed unable to concentrate.

Could she be lovesick? Juliet remembered only too keenly what it was like to be ignored by or separated from the object of her devotion. She shivered. Her own illusions had been shattered to devastating effect before she even reached her nineteenth birthday and she hoped Selina would never have to endure that.

The temptation to ask if something had happened in London was strong, but she had no right to pry, unless the girl chose to confide in her. Since Selina was officially 'out', she had no further need of a governess and it was her mother to whom she ought to turn if something was troubling her.

'I hope to have finished mending your gown soon.' As Juliet spoke, the sound of the schoolroom piano, somewhat stumblingly played, drifted through the wall. She rose. 'I'll go and tell Amy to stop if it's making your headache worse.'

'No, don't. I — like to hear people nearby. It doesn't bother me.'

'Well, if you're sure . . . Perhaps I'd better go back to her and leave you to rest.'

Selina smiled and for a moment the tiredness lifted from her eyes.

'Miss Radley?'

'Yes?'

'No, nothing.'

Juliet hesitated a moment longer, but when Selina said no more, she forced herself to return to the schoolroom. She glanced around with some trepidation, expecting to find some sign of misdeeds carried out in her absence.

11

Amy did not even seem aware of her, so absorbed was she in her practising. The music was now beginning to flow more smoothly and expressively, despite the occasional little mistake. While she seemed so diligent, Juliet did not like to interrupt her and she picked up her sewing again. The music stopped.

'Miss Radley?'

'Yes?'

'I'm — I'm sorry for what I said. You're not cross with me, are you?'

Her eyes gazed at Juliet like a puppy's from beneath her unruly hair.

'No, I'm not cross,' Juliet replied. 'But mark my words, young lady, unless you learn to curb your outspokenness, you will find yourself in deep trouble one day.'

'Then why did God give me a tongue, if I'm not allowed to use it?'

Juliet gave her a conspiratorial look.

'That's for after you're married and do exactly what you please.'

★   ★   ★

'Then you will be on your best behaviour tonight?' Juliet urged her pupil one last time, knowing that it would be she and not Amy, who would bear the brunt of Mrs Gibson's displeasure if the girl did anything outrageous.

'I'll be a perfect angel,' Amy promised, clasping her hands to her breast and smiling seraphically.

'I don't expect miracles.'

They made their way down the narrow flight of stairs to the first floor and then along the landing towards the grand staircase, which swept into the marble entrance hall. Behind them their long trains whispered along the carpeted treads.

Voices were audible from behind the closed doors of the dining-room. It was only on rare occasions that Juliet was invited to join the Gibsons and their guests for meals, usually when it was necessary to make up numbers because someone had been unable to attend at the last minute, or, once, so that there would not be thirteen to dinner.

The drawing-room was still empty. Juliet took her customary seat in the darkest corner of the room, farthest from the empty fireplace. Mrs Gibson insisted that the governess should stay downstairs with her pupils, ostensibly so she could accompany them on the piano when they sang. Much was made in society of Mrs Gibson's generosity in permitting her governess to be present on such occasions, even if she took no part in the conversation. Only Mrs Gibson and Juliet knew that she had an ulterior motive.

They had not long to wait before they heard a door, followed by merry voices, the rustle of silk and taffeta and the creak of whalebone. Governess and pupil rose politely and Amy stepped forward to be kissed and made a fuss of. As the ladies settled like butterflies on the couches and armchairs, Juliet noticed that Selina seemed to have brightened in the presence of her friends.

Ignored, isolated, Juliet often wished that she might be allowed to remain in the privacy of the schoolroom. Only fragments of conversation drifted in her direction as she was too far away from most of the speakers.

It felt like a very long time before the gentlemen joined them. Most of the guests were familiar to Juliet from previous visits, but even if it had not been so, she would have been able to identify Captain Gibson.

His upright bearing betrayed his military background, though he was in civilian dress on this occasion. He was not in the first flush of youth and years spent abroad on active service had aged him, adding faint lines across his high, broad forehead and around his eyes and mouth. His skin was lightly tanned by exposure to hotter climes and keen grey eyes seemed to take in the whole room.

On the whole, he was a handsome man, taller, leaner and more athletic than his cousin, George Gibson, who, with his comfortable life as a country squire, had begun to accumulate a little additional weight to his already stocky figure.

There was not much time for Juliet to make observations. She was called upon by Mrs Gibson to accompany her two pupils, who sang a duet for the company. Selina seemed rather shy at first, but Amy relished her moment of glory.

On her way back to her seat, Juliet couldn't help overhearing Mrs Gibson's reply to some comment.

'Oh, yes, we are so fortunate in Miss Radley. She is such a bluestocking, I am almost afraid my daughters will become too learned.'

Juliet flushed, knowing she was meant to hear. Once, when she had just begun to work for the Gibsons, she had made the mistake of suggesting an answer to a question being debated by the company at large. A subsequent consultation on a book on the subject had proved she was correct.

Mrs Gibson had never forgiven her

for that and seemed to take pleasure in demonstrating on every occasion that Juliet Radley might well be clever, but it was she, Henrietta Gibson, who had a wealthy husband, a beautiful house, two pretty daughters and everything else the heart could desire.

'As long as a lady doesn't become a dull pendant, I don't believe it is possible for her to become too learned.'

The voice was deep and resonant, though it was not raised. Juliet glanced instinctively at the speaker. Captain Gibson was smiling politely at his cousin's wife.

'Ah, I wish there were more gentlemen who agreed with you,' Mrs Gibson replied, visibly flustered, 'but I must think of the marriage prospects of my daughters.'

'And anyway,' Amy couldn't help butting in, 'if you say things like that, Miss Radley will make me work twice as hard, and I don't want to.'

'Amy!' her mother exclaimed, scandalised.

But Captain Gibson laughed and called Amy over to sit beside him.

Juliet noticed that Amy seemed to be studying her second cousin intently. Obviously it did not escape Captain Gibson's notice either.

'Is anything the matter?' he asked.

'Oh, well, you know, I thought you'd be wearing your smart red coat,' Amy confessed artlessly.

Captain Gibson smiled. It was a pleasant smile that illuminated his rather grave features.

'I'm on half-pay now. My regiment was disbanded soon after the peace treaty was signed. In any case, those red coats are not half so smart after they've been drenched with rain, mud and blood.'

Amy's eyes widened.

'Blood?' she repeated. 'Were you injured, then, sir?' She added the last word as an afterthought.

Juliet noticed the way the smile crinkled the corners of the captain's eyes. Many people were annoyed by

18

Amy's questions or only gave her flippant answers. She simply refused to understand that as a child, and a female at that, it was her place to listen and answer rather than take the lead in conversation.

'There are few officers with any courage who have not been wounded,' he replied.

'Why?'

'Because the enemy will always concentrate their fire on the officers in the hopes that if the men are left without leaders, they will panic and flee.'

'That's not fair,' Amy declared.

'We do the same to them.'

'Do you? Oh, well, then I suppose . . . ' She trailed away and seemed to consider his answer for a moment.

Juliet glanced around. Mrs Gibson was fortunately occupied and in the buzz of conversation had apparently not heard Amy's questions, because otherwise she would have undoubtedly called her daughter away.

Amy, undeterred, picked up her earlier thread. 'But were you ever injured?'

'A few times. None very grave, fortunately. Sometimes, if you are far enough away, the bullet is already spent and though it stings, it causes no more than a bruise, as if you had fallen from your horse.'

Several more questions followed. Captain Gibson did not treat Amy like a baby, something Juliet knew the girl appreciated, but the governess suspected that he was not telling her the full truth either.

Amy seemed utterly absorbed in his narrative and she cast a look of irritation at her mother when Mrs Gibson suggested it was high time for her to retire for the night.

'Please, Mamma, just five minutes more.' Puppy eyes were turned lugubriously upwards. 'I'm not the least bit tired.'

'You have monopolised Captain Gibson far too long as it is.'

'I don't mind,' the captain began, but Mrs Gibson was not to be shaken.

'It is already past her usual hour and she will be tearful and bad-tempered if she doesn't have enough sleep.' Mrs Gibson cast a severe look at Juliet, who had risen, knowing she too would be banished to the upper regions of the house. 'I'm surprised you have not seen to the child already, Miss Radley.'

Juliet knew it would have been a mistake to answer back, though the temptation was strong. Nor could she confess that she too had become absorbed and lost track of time. She curtsied in silence and attempted to look suitably penitent.

Amy opened her mouth, but obviously thought better of making a fuss. At her mother's bidding, she made her curtseys and bade everyone goodnight. Before she joined Juliet, who was waiting by the door, Amy darted back to Captain Gibson and hastily pecked him on the cheek.

'I'm glad you weren't badly injured,'

she declared and scuttled out of the room, cheeks crimson at her own daring.

Juliet saw the bemusement in the captain's face as she drew the door shut behind them. Mrs Gibson began apologising for her younger child and though she could not make out his words, Juliet could tell Captain Gibson was reassuring her.

Then she turned her attention to her charge, agreeing with her that Captain Gibson did indeed seem very nice and no doubt looked very handsome in his uniform, and it was unfair that they should be sent upstairs so soon.

But for all her complaints, Amy almost always slept the sleep of the righteous. Having crammed the day with as much adventure and excitement as she could, she instantly tumbled into sleep in as headlong a fashion as she did everything else.

It was Juliet who was left to sit in her own room, listening for Selina, thinking with a smile of Captain Gibson's kindness to Amy, though she was well aware that neither he nor anyone else had noticed that she, Juliet Radley, had been there, nor would miss her now she was gone.

★ ★ ★

It was still dark when Juliet woke, her heart racing, oddly convinced that something was amiss. The curtains at the window were not quite closed and a long ray of moonlight stretched across the room.

Perhaps it was nothing more than that, she thought. She closed her eyes and snuggled down again. Then she heard it.

Rustle, rustle, rustle. And then the soft padding of bare feet along the passage outside her room. Juliet's eyes sprang open. Had Amy had a nightmare? On increasingly rare occasions, the girl would wake her and crawl into bed with her and they would discuss her dreams in whispers.

23

But the steps went on, past her room towards the landing. Juliet slid out of bed, thoroughly awake now. Though it was a close night, she felt a chill deep inside her. She reached for the gown she had discarded before going to bed and pulled it on over her shift like a dressing-gown, though she did not attempt to fasten the bodice. She edged the door open. All was silent. But still she had to set her mind at rest.

Silence reigned in the girls' room. Juliet stole across to the bed. Amy was curled up on her side, her covers half-kicked away, one bare foot gleaming in the moonlight. Juliet breathed a sigh of relief. She had been mistaken. It must have been her imagination, or some other noise she had misinterpreted.

Then she glanced across to Selina's side of the bed. The covers were thrown back and there was an indentation in the pillow. But Selina was gone.

For a long moment, Juliet stared at the empty space, fear rising in her throat. Keep calm, she told herself. Nothing can happen to her in her own home. She's only gone to fetch something from the schoolroom, or she's restless because she can't sleep.

Juliet hurried across the room, closing the door as softly as her haste would allow. Despite the fact she had heard footsteps move towards the stairs, she could not resist glancing into the schoolroom. It was empty.

She would have expected such a prank from Amy. But not from Selina, not at her age, not with guests in the house. Perhaps she had gone to gossip secretly with one of her friends.

Drawing her gown tighter round herself, Juliet felt her way along the passage and down the stairs. Every noise seemed to be magnified, the rustle of her gown, the thudding of her heart, the creak of the stairs, the slap of her bare feet on the floor.

The first floor landing was startlingly bright in comparison with the rest of the house. Light from the full moon streamed in through an uncurtained window at the head of the stairs. Nothing moved, nothing stirred. As she crept past the closed doors, she could not hear a single whisper or girlish giggle.

If Selina had come this way, where had she gone? Who would she go to? Or could she be downstairs? A floorboard shrieked beneath her foot and Juliet stopped, heart pounding. She wanted to run, and yet she was afraid of rousing the house. If it was some harmless prank, she did not want Selina to get into trouble. But if she was in some kind of danger . . .

The silent, dark house frightened her. The chill was seeping into her bones. She would have to go downstairs to make certain Selina was not there. But as Juliet began to move, she suddenly heard a door click behind her.

'Who's there?' a masculine voice whispered.

She whisked round. In the moonlight she could see the outline of a man, not ten paces away from her, and the gleam of a pistol in his hand.

2

For two heartbeats, Juliet could do nothing but stare. Then the silhouette moved a step closer into a shaft of light. A tiny sound escaped her.

It was Captain Gibson, dressed only in his nightshirt and dressing gown.

'Who's there?' he repeated.

'I — it's Miss Radley, the governess.' Her throat was so dry, she could hardly speak. Instinctively she moved out of the shadows so he could see her better, though she clutched her gown closed at her breast at the same time.

He had lowered the pistol as he approached, even seemed a little abashed by it.

'What are you doing up at this hour?' he asked. 'Is anything wrong?'

'Selina's not in her bed. I heard a noise and went to look . . . '

Her explanation was cut short. They

both distinctly heard a door thud downstairs. A stray strand of hair fluttered across Juliet's face as Captain Gibson strode past her towards the head of the stairs. Juliet followed. She felt both safer and more exposed now she was not alone. If they should be caught together in this state . . .

Neither of them spoke as they descended into the hall. The marble floor was icy after the carpeted stairs. Captain Gibson paused, but Juliet had caught sight of something. Afraid to speak, she tugged his sleeve to attract his attention and pointed. The drawing room door was ajar.

He mouthed something at her, perhaps 'wait here', but she wasn't willing to be left behind. The gentlest touch made the door waft open, whispering across the carpet. Beyond Captain Gibson's shoulder, Juliet caught sight of a tall, ghostly figure floating towards them.

'Selina?' the captain whispered.

There was no response. The figure

continued moving towards them. There could be no doubt about its identity, however. Juliet slipped past her companion to take the girl by both shoulders.

'Selina, what are you doing here? You gave me such a fr — '

The last word died on her lips. Selina's eyes were half open, but glazed, sightless.

'She's sleep-walking,' Juliet said, turning towards Captain Gibson. She was trying to reassure herself as much as anything else.

'Best not wake her then,' he replied. 'Has she done this before?'

'Not to my knowledge and I've been here three years.'

The girl had stopped in her tracks at Juliet's touch.

'We'd best get her back to bed before she catches a chill.'

After a split second's hesitation, Captain Gibson removed his dressing gown and threw it round Selina's shoulders. Fortunately the darkness hid their self-conscious blushes as they moved on together. The grand staircase and the landing were wide enough for all three to walk abreast. Selina was perfectly compliant, going wherever they guided her.

'You'd best go first.' Captain Gibson breathed the words as they reached the foot of the second staircase.

Juliet nodded. She took Selina by the hand to lead the way, while the captain brought up the rear. Amy fortunately was still asleep as they tiptoed into the room. Juliet removed the dressing gown and Selina clambered back into bed of her own volition.

'Thank you for your help,' Juliet whispered, holding out the dressing gown to him.

Captain Gibson shrugged. 'I seem to have done very little,' he replied. 'I'm sorry if I frightened you. Force of habit. The slightest noise is enough to wake me and,' he twisted the pistol ruefully in his hand, 'I never sleep without a weapon close at hand.'

They were standing outside Juliet's room now, very close together so they would not have to raise their voices. In the darkness, Juliet was aware of his scent, his sheer masculine presence, taller and broader than her in his full, white nightshirt.

'At least we need not fear burglars,' she said, hoping a joke would break the tension, but blushing fiercely nonetheless.

Perhaps he smiled back. In the dark it was difficult to tell.

'Goodnight Miss — Radley, is it?'

She curtsied and bowed her head.

'Goodnight, sir.'

She slid round the door and listened to the stairs creak beneath his weight. Juliet shivered, then crept across the room and in between her cool sheets.

The whole episode had been unnerving. Selina's uncharacteristic behaviour suggested that Juliet had been right to worry about the girl. And then there was the sudden intimacy she was thrown into with Captain Gibson.

She had allowed herself to think about him before she fell asleep, despite knowing she was an old maid and would always remain so because of her past. She had been so certain Captain Gibson would never notice her; she would never speak to him, unless he spoke to her first; he would scarcely be aware of her name.

And nothing has changed, she told herself firmly. Tomorrow he will behave as if none of this happened and I will do my duty and keep silent. And yet she felt a ripple of sensation run through her as, unbidden, the image of Captain Gibson floated before her closed eyes.

'Well, Miss Radley, what is it now?'

She makes it sound as if I made a habit of disturbing her before breakfast, Juliet thought. Every line in Mrs Gibson's body showed her impatience. She was seated at her dressing table, her body half-twisted towards Juliet, a vial of perfume clutched in her hand.

Juliet glanced at the lady's maid, who was fussing with the morning dishabille her mistress intended to don presently. But Mrs Gibson showed no sign of dismissing the maid.

'It's about Miss Gibson,' Juliet began.

She had come to the conclusion that it was her duty to inform Selina's mother of her nocturnal activities. She had decided, however, to say nothing about Captain Gibson's presence at the scene and hope that he would not mention it of his own accord and so make it look as if she had something to hide.

'Miss Gibson is no concern of yours any more. It is Miss Amy you are employed to teach.'

'I understand that, madam. I only wished to inform you that — that I found Miss Gibson sleepwalking last night. I fear she may have some secret sorrow or — '

She got no further. Mrs Gibson had grown redder and redder during her speech and now cut her short.

'That's enough, Miss Radley. I'll

attend to the matter. You may go now.'

Juliet obeyed, more than a little stunned. She had expected that her mistress would deny that Selina was prone to such behaviour, or that at very least she would ask for more information about where and how she had discovered Selina wandering.

Perhaps Selina had done this before, when she was younger. Perhaps there was nothing wrong after all. Clearly Mrs Gibson resented what she took to be a covert criticism of her maternal care for her oldest child.

But Amy was waiting upstairs and there was no time for any more speculation.

★　★　★

On the crest of the hill, Richard Gibson brought his horse to a standstill so he could survey the beloved, much-missed scene. It was a long time since he had been to Winfield Hall and it seemed to him he had forgotten the freshness of the air, the rippling birdsong in the hedgerows, the greenness of the vegetation. He breathed in the scent of newly mown hay and memories of the stench of blood, gunpowder, infection and decay seemed to fade in his mind, as if they were nightmares and now at last he had woken up.

As a boy he had often come to stay with his cousin, George. The two of them had roamed the woods, meadows and country lanes together, climbing trees, drinking from streams when they were thirsty, feasting on wild strawberries or blackberries, depending on how far the season was advanced. And at night they had slept, exhausted, in the same room now shared by Selina and Amy.

His stallion danced and flicked his ears. Richard slapped him gently on the neck.

'Steady, old fellow.'

The fineness of the morning had tempted him to ride out alone, without even telling George where he was going. But it could not last much longer. A change in the light told him, even without consulting his watch, that it was time to turn back if he did not want to be late dressing for dinner and so incur the reproachful looks of Henrietta, who seemed determined to pair him off with one of the single maidens staying at the hall.

It was not even that he was a particularly good catch. Only the son of the younger of two brothers, a half-pay captain with no regiment of his own, much less any hope of promotion now the war was over. Besides which, he felt far too old to have much in common with the young girls he had been introduced to the previous evening. But he was a Gibson and Henrietta felt she had a duty to fulfil.

Richard urged the black stallion into a steady trot. The motion of the horse and the fresh summer breeze made the skirts of his coat flap and lift as he bounded along.

In between memories of his youth, he

found himself thinking of more recent events, most notably the incident during the night. He was still somewhat embarrassed by the fact he had overreacted so badly to the sound of footsteps in the dark. He was fortunate the governess was not the nervous, hysterical type, who might have screamed the house down or fainted at the sight of a weapon.

To add to his embarrassment, he had very little idea what the governess looked like, apart from a nebulous figure in the darkness. He knew she had been present in the drawing room after dinner the previous evening, but he had paid scant attention.

She had not even been properly introduced to him, he realised, which had made the scene on the staircase all the more awkward. There had been references to Miss Radley at dinner and the tiresomeness of governesses in general, a favourite theme of Henrietta's. But being a childless, penniless bachelor, such comments had floated over his head as utterly irrelevant to his current situation.

He was not far from the octagonal gatehouse that marked the drive of Winfield Hall when he spotted two figures on the dusty road. The smaller one was dressed all in white, apart from a bright blue sash that matched the blue ribbons of her wide-brimmed hat.

But it was to her companion that his eye was drawn. Her plain, dark gown and unadorned hat told him this must be the governess. He didn't know whether he wanted to seek her out or to avoid her, but the decision was taken out of his hands. At the sound of hooves, they both turned inwards to glance back and Amy's face blossomed into a smile.

'Captain Gibson!'

He urged his mount on to catch up with them. They waited for him, but the governess lowered her head so the brim of her hat hid her eyes and cheeks and left him only with the tantalising glimpse of a shapely pair of lips, pressed lightly together. A mouth that seemed to invite kisses.

There was little time to think of such things. Unable to restrain her impatience any longer, Amy ran a few steps to meet him. She tilted her head back to look up at him, clutching the crown of her hat with one hand to prevent it from sliding from her head.

'Good morning,' he said to both of them. 'You've been out walking, I see.'

'Yes, sir. We're going home now to get dressed for dinner,' Amy replied.

One eye peeped at him from beneath the brim of Miss Radley's hat. It was enough to decide him. Richard unhooked his foot from his stirrup and dropped down beside his horse.

'So am I. Perhaps we can walk together.'

Amy was enthusiastic and Miss Radley made no objection. So the little procession took shape, with Richard leading his horse by the reins, Amy dancing alongside him and the governess gliding at a more sedate pace beside her. Whenever he looked at the girl, Richard inevitably glimpsed Miss Radley as well.

Amy prattled cheerfully about all she had seen that morning, apparently oblivious to the awkwardness between the adults, and Richard parried her questions as best he could. They reached the gates and turned into the drive.

'If you please, sir,' Amy suddenly spoke up, 'how should I address you? 'Sir' seems so cold and 'Captain Gibson' is so formal, and you are a close relative after all.'

'Not so close to you as to your father. And I suspect your mother would prefer things to remain formal between us.'

Amy pulled a face.

'But perhaps you'd better call me Cousin Richard when no one else is nearby,' he added on impulse.

'Oh, thank you, Cousin Richard.' Amy availed herself of his permission at once, then spoilt the effect completely by adding, 'It's not a very pretty name, though, is it?'

'I'm not sure boys are supposed to have pretty names,' Richard replied, amused.

'Oh, you know what I mean. Don't you agree with me, Miss Radley?'

The governess flushed at this unexpected appeal. In the past minutes, Richard had got a closer look at her face. She was not exactly conventionally pretty, with her almond-shaped eyes and light brown hair the colour of a mallard duck's wing, but her face was arresting because it was so expressive.

'It's really not for me to say.'

'Oh, you must have an opinion, surely,' Amy exclaimed in exasperation.

Richard wondered whether he ought to chide her, but Miss Radley forestalled him.

'Very well, then, Amy, I think Richard is a plain, sensible, manly name and nobody need be ashamed of it.'

But she blushed even more fiercely and fixed her eyes on the road ahead.

Amy pouted, but did not seem unduly put out.

'I'm glad you approve of my name,' Richard said, wanting to coax a few more words out of the governess. 'Might I ask what name your parents gave you?'

The blush grew more intense, but it was Amy who replied.

'Oh, she won't tell you. I've asked her a dozen times and she refuses. I know it begins with J, because her initials are embroidered on the corner of her handkerchiefs.'

'Then it shouldn't be so hard to guess,' Richard suggested.

'I've asked and asked her and I'm sure I've got the right name, but she says no to all my suggestions. She says it isn't Jane or Joan or Joanna or Julia or Juliana or Jemima or Judith or — ' Amy rolled her eyes, obviously hunting for more names.

'I'm sure Miss Radley has her reasons.' He searched for something to divert her. Miss Radley's cheeks were still burning. 'Isn't that a blue butterfly over there?'

'Where? Oh, I see it.' Amy began to chase after it.

Richard called after her, 'Gently does it. Don't frighten it or you'll never be able to get close.'

The girl paid no heed to his words and dashed off, despite the heat, leaving the two adults to bring up the rear.

'I'm sorry if — '

'Thank you for — '

They both spoke at once, stopped and exchanged smiles and fleeting glances. No, Miss Radley was not pretty, and yet that smile made her beautiful.

'Ladies first.'

'Oh, no, I merely wanted to thank you for keeping Amy occupied.'

'Think nothing of it. One of the marks of a good officer is knowing where best to deploy your troops,' he replied, watching Amy stalking the butterfly, only to have it fly off as she had almost reached it. 'If Amy were a boy, she would be perfect for the light infantry, small, quick and intelligent, and, I imagine, a deadly shot if her questions are anything to go by. She'd make an excellent scout, to make note of the terrain and the positions of any potential enemies she may stumble across.'

'Enemies.' Miss Radley laughed. 'I didn't know we had any of those.'

'One cannot be too careful.' But the joke had run its course and he searched for a different topic. 'It seems odd that Amy has grown so big. She was only five when I last saw her.'

'A few more years and I shall have to look for a new position,' the governess agreed. 'It makes me feel old, to think that she and Selina are almost old enough to be married.' The mention of her former pupil made Miss Radley frown suddenly. 'I — I told Mrs Gibson that I found Selina sleepwalking,' she added, 'but I made no mention of your presence. I hope that was correct?'

'Yes, I think so,' he said. 'I'm glad

you warned me.'

They walked on a little further in silence. The horse's hooves thudded dully on the dry ground. Amy appeared to be talking to the butterfly, coaxing it to sit still until she could get close enough to examine it.

'I really ought to rejoin my pupil.'

'Yes, I suppose so. Miss Radley?' She paused and Richard forced himself on before he could have second thoughts. 'I couldn't help wondering — has Amy ever guessed your name correctly?'

'No, not yet, not quite.'

'Would you have any objection to telling me?'

She hesitated.

'I promise not to laugh,' he assured her, hoping she would not launch something too bizarre at him.

'You promise not to tell Amy?'

'You have my oath as a gentleman.'

'Well, then — it's Juliet.'

'Oh — ah,' he stammered. 'That's rather pretty.'

'You think so? I have an elderly aunt

who never calls me anything but Jane and repeats a thousand times a day that no good ever came of giving a girl a romantic name.' Though she was laughing, he could see a shadow of pain in her eyes. 'She said it would make me think I was a heroine and would ruin me utterly.'

Something prevented him from commenting on her last words. She blushed again, apparently conscious that she had said too much.

'I can see why you have to keep it a secret from Amy. If she knew, she would be constantly declaiming 'Romeo, Romeo, wherefore art thou Romeo' while you were trying to teach her.'

'Quite so.'

Juliet felt happier than she had for a long time as she sat in the drawing room, listening to the other ladies gossiping and Amy offering her opinion when it wasn't wanted. She couldn't help hoping that when the gentlemen joined them, Captain Gibson would perhaps meet her gaze briefly and acknowledge her presence with a nod or a smile. She had no right to expect anything more than that, and yet . . .

And yet every single night since his arrival nearly two weeks previously, he had found some excuse to sit close to her, ostensibly to talk to Amy, though he never failed to draw Juliet into the conversation too. Not only that, but he had on several occasions 'chanced' to meet them while they were out on their daily walk. There were even times when Juliet forgot she was no longer at home and, as the daughter of a clergyman, one of the more important ladies in the parish.

She jumped as the door opened. Surely it was still far too early for the gentlemen? And indeed it was only the footman, bearing a card on a silver platter.

'A gentleman to see you, madam.'

A glance at the card seemed to suffice.

'Oh, show him in by all means,' Mrs

Gibson exclaimed, undisguised pleasure illuminating her still pretty face. The servant withdrew and she added almost to herself, 'I wonder what can bring him to this backwater?'

She had risen and Juliet saw her glance at her reflection in the mirror and pat her curls hastily. Then she sailed across the room to meet the unexpected guest, her train sweeping behind her like a peacock's tail.

There was a bustle and a stir among the other ladies too.

'My dear, Mrs Gibson, how good of you to receive me like this. You must forgive me for arriving unannounced at such an hour. I could not resist the temptation to pay my respects to you at the very first opportunity . . . '

Mrs Gibson's gracious reply blurred in Juliet's ears. She thought she had forgotten that voice. But the instant she heard it, the hair rose on the back of her neck. All the anguish she thought she had forgotten flooded through her.

It can't be him. It cannot be. You are imagining it.

But when she forced herself to raise her eyes, she saw that familiar figure, the set of his shoulders, the turn of his head as he gazed down at his hostess and gallantly raised her hand to his lips in a gesture Juliet remembered only too well.

So many years had passed and she had felt she had grown old. But he scarcely looked any older, apart from perhaps a hint of tiredness about his eyes.

Then he turned towards Selina, took her hand, bowed and murmured something with that irresistible smile that Juliet had once thought was reserved for her alone. She saw the radiant look that transformed Selina's face. She had sometimes glimpsed that same look in the mirror as she flew by, a light-footed girl of eighteen, ignorant of the cruelties of men.

The newcomer turned his eyes in Juliet's direction, as if he sensed her gaze across the width of the room. She flinched, but forced herself not to look away. She realised she had hoped that she was wrong, that this was some other man, so similar to Hugh Faversham that he might be mistaken for his twin.

His gaze was cool, hard, indifferent, appraising Juliet as if she were merely part of the furniture. But no, there could be no mistake. Mrs Gibson called him by name and drew him away to be introduced to the other guests. In her dark corner Juliet was left with the humiliating realisation.

She might remember every detail about Hugh Faversham and what he had once been to her. But he remembered neither her face nor her name.

3

The evening dragged nightmarishly long. Never had Juliet so longed for escape. Voices blended and swirled around her. She did not even notice when the gentlemen entered or if Captain Gibson had so much as glanced in her direction.

She had thought that if she had ever met Hugh Faversham again, and that was highly unlikely, she would be able to lift her chin, give him a long, indifferent stare and say something cutting and witty that would prove she was no longer the innocent dupe she had once been.

She had told herself that by then she would have achieved something and she would be able to prove to Faversham that he had not succeeded in ruining her life. Sometimes she had even dared to dream she would make some splendid match that would set her far above Faversham so she could gaze down at him with a sort of indulgent contempt and that he would wince and squirm like the worm he was.

But the truth was that the dream, like so many she had cherished in her youth, had never been likely to be fulfilled. Even if she had never met Hugh Faversham and burnt up in his flames like a moth in a candle, her marriage prospects had never been spectacular.

She was the oldest daughter of a family of six and her father had been the parson of an obscure country parish, some miles north of Nottingham. They did not meet many people of their own class, except when they managed to get to the Nottingham Races or the Assembly, or perhaps a concert or play.

Juliet had read novels about girls travelling to London or Bath or other fashionable resorts, but there was not enough money for that and the boys' education too, and she had no rich patroness who would have been willing to take her under her wing.

It was at the Nottingham Races that she first met Faversham. That in itself ought to have told her something about his character. He had literally bumped into her mother, apologised and offered to find them the best places available. Juliet was still not certain if the meeting was contrived or accidental.

She was pretty sure, however, that Faversham had deliberately sought her out at the Assembly that evening. Perhaps he mistook her shyness for pride. Or perhaps he was flattered by the obvious awe in her eyes as she gazed up at his flawlessly handsome face.

'Miss Radley,' he said, bowing over her hand, and she had thought she had never liked the sound of her name so well.

As he straightened up, she was lost in those mischievous blue eyes. Nothing else existed in the world. He smiled, revealing beautifully even, white teeth.

She could scarcely believe it when he asked her to be his partner for the country-dances.

She had known at the time that she was awkward and shy during those precious minutes while they stood out at the top or bottom or the longways set, but it didn't seem to worry him. He joked and flirted and flattered her and long before the evening was over, she had told him the secret of her first name.

'Juliet,' he repeated. 'Sweet Juliet, fair Juliet. No other name could suit you half so well.'

All too soon, the Radleys had been forced to leave. Mr Radley was not a well man and their journey home was a long and arduous one. Faversham had made himself agreeable to her parents and escorted them to their hired carriage to help Juliet inside, and thus it was he had received an invitation to call at the parsonage if he ever found himself in the neighbourhood.

Juliet could still remember vividly the

journey home, the sleepless night that followed, the mixture of languor, longing and dreamy contentment with which she had picked over her breakfast.

Unable to concentrate on her reading, she had taken up her sewing and seated herself by the open parlour window. The mechanical work required little thought and she was free to reminisce and to weave bright dreams about the future. And then, in the midst of this, she was interrupted by a dulcet voice.

'*But soft! What light through yonder window breaks?*

It is the east, and Juliet is the sun.'

Startled, she turned to the window and found those blue eyes and white teeth twinkling at her from beneath the brim of a tricorn hat.

'*Arise, fair sun, and kill the envious moon,*

Who is already sick and pale with grief,

That thou her maid are far more fair than she:

But not her maid, since she is envious,

Her vestal livery is but sick and green,

And none but fools do wear it.'

She was tongue-tied, flattered that he had learnt so much by rote, simply to play on her name. It was not till much later that she saw the hidden meaning in his words.

She knew it was the custom for gentlemen to call upon their dancing partners, to make sure they had not caught the obligatory cold that young ladies were supposedly susceptible to catching in overheated ballrooms, but Juliet had hardly dared hope that Faversham would come.

Her parents welcomed him and he talked entertainingly to them, but Juliet felt his secret glances were for her alone. Her father was a sociable man, sometimes too much so when he extended hospitality they could ill afford or monopolised guests, oblivious to the possibility that they might prefer to speak to someone else.

One visit led to another. Faversham was staying with a friend nearby. He had only intended to stay in Nottinghamshire for a week during the races, but, he told Juliet in confidential tones when they managed to find a moment alone, he found himself unable to leave.

Faversham called as frequently as he dared, often timing his visits to coincide with her father's absences. Or sometimes he intercepted Juliet while she was out walking with her younger siblings.

On one such occasion, when the children had run on ahead, around a bend in the road, Faversham pretended that a gust of wind had blown grit in his eye. Juliet could not credit her naivety now, but she had stretched up on tiptoe to try to help him and he had scooped her into the crook of his arm and kissed her firmly, passionately and all too briefly on the lips.

He had, of course, been extremely apologetic afterwards.

'It was wicked of me to take advantage of your trusting nature, but indeed I couldn't help myself, you looked so enchanting,' he said, touching her cheek lightly. 'Do you say you forgive me.'

And of course she had, though she had been longing for him to repeat his trespass so she might forgive him again. But he had been too wily for that and the children were within earshot and likely to notice their absence soon.

It struck Juliet that Faversham had hooked her, teased her and reeled her in as he might have landed a valuable fish. And when he was certain her affections were engaged, he had grown distant and melancholy and she had had to coax him before he confessed what troubled him.

By then he had persuaded her to meet him in secret. She knew it was wrong, that every meeting risked exposure and the ruin of her good name. But she had no other means of speaking to him in private.

That night they had met in the

orchard at the far end of the garden. Faversham had leapt the wall that separated the parsonage grounds from the graveyard, murmuring,

'With love's light wings did I o'er-perch these walls,

For stony limits cannot hold love out;

And what love can do, that dares love attempt.'

But having quoted this snatch of Shakespeare, he lapsed into gloom until she wheedled him into speaking out.

'I wish — I wish I was more worthy of your love and could shower you with jewels and silks and lace and all the luxuries you deserve.'

'But I don't want those things. All I want is you.'

'Bless you, my darling.' He kissed her lingeringly, then wrenched himself away. 'No, I cannot do it. Oh, if I had not wasted so much of my patrimony in idleness and vanity, I might have been able to marry you . . . But your father would never consent to let you marry a man so little capable of taking care of you.'

She had protested, told him her father was not worldly or ambitious, that she was used to leading a simple life, that she was sure something could be salvaged from his fortune if he was careful and that her father might be able to settle a small sum of money on her, though she did not dare tell him it was unlikely to be more than £50, for fear of frightening him off.

And then he had drawn her into his arms and blessed her again and kissed her and the scent of apples hung in the warm, late summer air and . . .

Juliet jerked, pushing the images aside, fighting them like a sleeper fights foul nightmares. The Gibsons' drawing room seemed so ordinary, so respectable. Mr Gibson was talking to his cousin, his arm around Amy, who was perched on the arm of her father's chair. Faversham was entertaining some of the ladies, including Selina and Mrs Gibson. As Juliet watched, the latter tapped Faversham lightly with her fan.

What would they think if they knew everything? Juliet closed her eyes for just a second and the images flashed across her inner eye, the agony of parting with Faversham, his promises to return as soon as he had put his affairs in some kind of order so he could speak to her father, the impossibility of corresponding because there was nobody to forward their letters in secret.

At first she was bolstered by memories. Only a week, he said, ten days. No more than that. She counted each day, each hour, believing each second was bringing them closer together. A week dragged past. Nothing. Eight days, nine days, ten days. Nothing.

She made excuses. Of course things had not been as simple as he had hoped, but he would come as soon as he could. He had given her his solemn oath, sworn it upon his life.

Two weeks, three weeks, a month. She couldn't sleep any more. Nothing tasted right. She hardly dared leave the house for fear he would arrive while she was away. Her mother hovered over her, anxious about her health. Surely Hugh could have found some means to send word to her. Surely he could have spared a few days to come and see her, to reassure her that, even if all had not been settled yet, he had begun his preparations and it would all turn out well in the end.

And then her fear had begun to rise, the black phantom she tried to fight away. He isn't like that. He loves me; he wouldn't desert me. Something must have happened to him. He is injured, ill, dead. She didn't even have an address where she might write to him, pleading for news. He cannot desert me; he would not. Not after all he said and did.

Six weeks, two months. And then there was that terrible day when the friend Faversham had been staying with in Nottinghamshire had dined at the parsonage at her father's invitation and

62

he mentioned he had received a letter.

'How is Faversham?' Mr Radley asked. 'I always liked the fellow.'

'Oh, in fine health. He's in Bath at present, has some hope of snaring an heiress . . . '

The pain was so searing, Juliet could not move from her seat, afraid she would faint. Her plate swam before her eyes and her mother, turning towards her, commented on her pallor.

'I don't feel well, Mamma. May I be excused?'

Her legs would scarcely bear her upright. The staircase was a sheer cliff. Only through an effort of will, she prevented herself from crawling up it. She had to be brave and strong until she reached her room. Only when she got there would she be able to let go. Her parents, the children, the servants must never know. Rain drummed on her window. She was being ripped apart, but nobody must ever know . . .

'Are you not well, Miss Radley?'

The words startled Juliet out of her

reverie. Captain Gibson was watching her with anxious eyes.

'I'm perfectly well, thank you.' She forced a smile to her lips.

If he knew everything, he would despise you, a cruel voice whispered in her ear.

Amy was saying goodnight and Juliet staggered to her feet, feeling as stiff as she had on that autumn afternoon when the truth about Faversham was finally brought home to her. Out of the corner of her eye, she watched him as she crossed the room, but he paid her no attention. As she was closing the door, however, she caught Captain Gibson's eye for an instant before she turned away.

Amy was excitable and naughty enough to keep Juliet occupied coaxing her and threatening her with dire punishments if she did not stop wasting time and get ready for bed. Not that Juliet was overly keen to be left alone with her thoughts. The longer she could prevent the dark cloud of memory from overshadowing her, the better.

Once Amy was in bed, she found herself sitting at the small window of her room, staring at the moon as it rose between the branches of the trees that overlooked the drive.

Every impulse in her body told her to run away from this place, away from Hugh Faversham. But she needed the money. Her brothers were only just starting to make their way in their chosen professions, her sisters newly married and living in straitened circumstances. Her youngest sister in particular was struggling, having married their father's last curate, who was now serving in the same capacity as Mr Radley's successor.

Their mother lived with first one, then another of her children, going wherever she was needed most, now looking after one of her daughters-in-law when she was in childbed, then going to help when someone else was taken sick.

A tap at the door interrupted her thought.

'Miss Radley?' It was Selina's voice.

Juliet tiptoed to the door. There was a feverish glitter in Selina's eyes.

'What is it?'

'Can I talk to you for a moment? I'm not the least bit sleepy, but I don't want to wake Amy. Besides which, she's only a child.'

Juliet couldn't help smiling at that. Selina was utterly unaware of how young and fragile she looked, despite being a full inch taller than her governess. Juliet stood aside and let her enter.

'Don't let Amy hear you say that.'

With a contented sigh, Selina let herself drop, face down, on to Juliet's bed.

'Isn't everything wonderful?' she sighed.

Juliet's cheek muscles froze as she attempted to smile. But Selina went on, relieving her of the need to find a suitable reply.

'London was exciting, but it's nice to be back home, away from the city smells. Now the guests have come, Mamma says we'll be able to go on jaunts and perhaps have a concert or a ball, and who knows what else.'

Her eyes took on a dreamy look Juliet recognised only too well. She was glad to see the girl looking so much happier, and yet she feared the cause of this transformation.

'Such a surprise, Mr Faversham turning up like that,' Selina gushed on, blushing in spite of her efforts not to. 'We met him in London, and he was so attentive — to Mamma, I mean, and he and Papa are capital friends, only some people say he is a sad rake, but he's always been so polite to us, and I'm sure the rumours must be exaggerated, don't you think?'

She raised her eyes in appeal. Juliet hesitated. She could see what Selina wanted her to say. She wanted to be told that rakes could be reformed by the love of a good woman and Juliet did not want to crush her like a butterfly.

Her instincts told her she must warn

the girl to stay away, not to play with fire for fear of scorching her wings. But how could she do it in a way Selina would take notice of, without revealing she had prior knowledge of Faversham? She wanted to stay out of his way, remain in the shadows where no one could see her, because one recollection might lead to another.

'You'd better be careful,' she said slowly. 'Rumour isn't always false and I would hate to see you have your heart broken like mine when I was not much older than you.'

Selina sat up, suddenly alert.

'You had a tragic romance? Tell me.'

Juliet laughed unconvincingly.

'Nothing much to tell — a very commonplace little tale. He made me believe he loved me and was going to marry me, and then he abandoned me.'

'And you have been pining for your lost love all these years?' Selina murmured sympathetically. 'Oh, poor Miss Radley.'

'No, I discovered long ago that that

man was not worthy of my tears. But for years afterwards, I couldn't trust any other man, and then my father died and I had to earn my own living.'

There was enough truth in the incomplete tale for it to be plausible. Selina did not need to know the rest. But Juliet was pretty sure it was all water off a duck's back. Selina was sympathetic, but wholly unconvinced that such a thing could happen to her too.

'Poor Miss Radley,' she repeated, scrambling up to hug her. 'I wish you could be as happy as I am now.'

'And I wish you could be as wise as I was after the event.'

Even this meant nothing to Selina, though she gave her solemn promise. Nothing could have shaken her confidence, except perhaps the full truth. But that was the one thing Juliet could not bring herself to tell her.

4

It was all very well for Juliet to resolve to keep a close eye on Selina, but it was not so easy to put into practice. Her duties kept her confined to the schoolroom for much of the day, apart from her daily walks with Amy, and even then they rarely met anyone. It was only in the evenings that she could observe the party as a whole, and only last thing at night and first thing in the morning that she saw Selina privately.

To make matters worse, Mrs Gibson had invited Faversham to stay at Winfield Hall and he had accepted. Nor did the Gibsons and their guests dine at home every night and when they were invited elsewhere, Juliet and Amy were left to entertain themselves all evening.

There was no further sleepwalking and Selina was utterly transformed from the pale, listless wraith she had been. She seemed to have wings on her heels and she chattered and laughed and sang more than usual.

Juliet was convinced Selina was in love as only a sheltered fifteen-year-old can be. All her impulses told her to voice her doubts to her employers. But if she had attempted to say anything to Mr Gibson, he would have looked blank, insisted that Selina was far too young for such nonsense and referred her hastily to his wife.

And Mrs Gibson had been glacial towards Juliet ever since the sleepwalking incident. Besides which, what could she say? I believe your daughter is in love with a man you have introduced her to and therefore presumably approve of, but who will break her heart and perhaps ruin her reputation? She had no evidence with which to support her allegations against Faversham and Mrs Gibson had made it abundantly clear that Selina was no longer Juliet's responsibility.

Amy did not make Juliet's life any

easier. The girl was unsettled, unable to concentrate because she knew there were guests in the house, some not much older than herself, who were enjoying themselves while she was expected to work. The hot weather did not help either, as it made sleeping difficult and made both pupil and teacher more fractious than usual.

Respite came from an unexpected source. One evening about a week after Faversham's arrival, Juliet had been listening in a desultory fashion to a discussion about an excursion that was planned for the following day, if the weather held fair.

'It sounds splendid, Henrietta,' Captain Gibson remarked, 'but I have a request.'

'Name it,' the hostess replied with her most ingratiating smile.

He glanced at Amy, who had recently taken to sitting on a footstool at his feet and leaning her arms or head against his knee when she grew tired.

'Would it incommode you terribly if

Amy came with us?'

'Oh, I don't know.' Mrs Gibson was flustered. 'She may find it dull — '

'No, I won't.'

'And Miss Radley could come too and keep Amy occupied and out of mischief,' Captain Gibson added, ignoring Amy's impetuous exclamation.

'Oh, but then we'll need two more seats in the carriage and I really don't think — '

'I don't mind riding,' Selina interrupted and reddened at the sound of her own voice. 'Amy could have my place in the landau.'

'And the governess can sit on the box with the coachman, can't she?' Mrs Tibbs suggested.

'But I want to ride on the box,' Amy intervened. 'Please, Mamma.'

Mrs Gibson's mouth twitched. It was never easy to resist Amy when she got that beseeching tone in her voice and that spaniel look in her eyes. Despite Juliet's best efforts, the wayward tress was drooping in her eyes again. It never ceased to amaze her that that lock didn't seem to trouble the girl at all.

'We'll see,' was all Mrs Gibson would vouchsafe, but Amy was shrewd enough to realise that, if she did not kick up a fuss, her mother almost certainly meant 'yes'.

She snuggled contentedly against her second cousin's knee and exchanged a conspiratorial wink with him. As Richard Gibson lifted his eyes, he caught Juliet looking at him and smiled at her in a way that made her smile back and then duck her head to hide the flush creeping over her cheeks.

★   ★   ★

Despite Amy's wheedling, it was Juliet who clambered, unaided, on to the box of the Gibsons' landau the following morning. Some of the younger ladies and all the gentlemen were accompanying them on horseback, even Colonel Halliday who, now she had seen him in broad daylight, Juliet suspected of being older than he appeared to be, though he was still very active and upright.

Juliet was not entirely sorry to be seated on the box. Her view of the countryside was unimpeded, save for the horses' heads in front of her. The movement of the carriage stirred the sluggish air into something resembling a breeze so that her hat ribbons fluttered. Unfortunately the wheels and hooves also churned up a fine dust, which covered her clothes and made her cough.

Even so, Juliet felt exhilaration growing inside her. Here she felt free for once, away from the confines of the schoolroom. The voices of the ladies in the carriage were tossed on the breeze, only stray phrases distinguishable above the thudding of hooves and the rhythmic wheezing of wheels. Amy's voice was one of the ones that drifted across to Juliet most often. She too seemed to relish her freedom.

Selina was part of the amorphous cluster of young riders, who sometimes paired off, then, when the width of the road permitted, might ride three or four abreast. The smaller groupings within the crowd constantly shifted and changed, though Faversham was never far from the ladies. Meanwhile Captain Gibson was riding side-by-side with the colonel, apparently deep in conversation.

They travelled through the undulating countryside, past fields, hop frames, meadows and woodland. In the distance a blue line of mountains was constantly visible, indicating where Wales lay. Although she had lived so long in Herefordshire, Juliet had seen little of the county, apart from the immediate vicinity of Winfield Hall and the nearest town, where on rare occasions she was permitted to accompany Mrs Gibson and her daughters when they went shopping.

So the first glimpse of the castle took her breath away, It stood on a hillock, nestling in the curve of the river. Solid stone walls reared up into the forget-me-not blue sky. It was only as they drew closer that it became obvious that apart from this façade, which had been left almost intact, the building was a roofless ruin.

Juliet had heard a great deal about this place. It had been a small Royalist garrison during the Civil War, which had held out as long as possible against a Parliamentarian siege and suffered the inevitable consequences when the war was over.

The landau and the cavalcade of horses passed across a sturdy stone bridge, guarded by the crumbling remains of what had obviously once been a redoubtable gatehouse. Juliet suspected the bridge was a modern structure, added for the convenience of sightseers, perhaps to replace a drawbridge.

There was a flurry as they drew to a standstill, the gentlemen dismounting hurriedly so they might assist the ladies. Juliet stared helplessly as Faversham placed himself beside Selina's horse and she slid gracefully down into his arms.

'Miss Radley.'

The voice was not loud, but it was close. Juliet started. Captain Gibson was standing beside the box of the landau, offering her his hand.

'May I help you?'

She flushed and glanced over her shoulder, but everyone seemed too preoccupied to notice.

'Thank you.'

Juliet gathered her petticoats together hastily before placing her hand in his. Captain Gibson gripped her fingers firmly. Self-conscious, she rushed her descent and tottered on reaching the ground.

'Steady there,' Captain Gibson murmured, catching her shoulder with his free hand.

Juliet's blush deepened. She could not look him in the eye, but she was acutely aware of his broad shoulders, only inches from her face.

'I'm sorry, sir, I — '

'There's no need to apologise.'

He had released her, but he was still

disturbingly close. She had a sudden flash of memory, remembering the glimpse through the darkness of his body clad in nothing but his nightshirt.

'Captain Gibson!'

He replied to the summons, but he managed to catch Juliet's eye for an instant before murmuring 'excuse me' and leaving her. Juliet compressed her lips. The time for daydreaming was over. Amy was weaving in and out of the crowd, getting in the way. Juliet took the shortest route to her charge and gripped her hand, though Amy protested that she was too old to be treated like a baby.

'Well then, be good,' Juliet murmured under her breath, 'unless you want your mamma to forbid us both from coming on any further excursions.'

The threat did the trick, at least for the moment. Amy was as docile as could reasonably be expected from someone with such a mercurial temperament.

Being so large, the party soon split

into smaller groups. Amy, pining for company near her own age, sidled up to Selina and the youngest of the Tibbs sisters, Catherine, who was a month or two younger than Selina. Only a few years ago, all three girls had played the same games and attended the same children's balls.

Inevitably Juliet was brought in closer proximity with Faversham than she had been for ten years. Her heartbeat quickened, but he did not even glance at her. The remainder of the little group consisted of Mrs Gibson, Captain Gibson and Miss Halliday, to whom the captain was explaining the history of the ruin.

Juliet would have liked to listen, but she dared not stray far from her charge and while Captain Gibson spoke softly, the rest of the party was loud in its merriment, encouraged by Faversham.

Juliet stiffened suddenly. As they wove between the half-demolished inner walls of the castle and peeped through the crumbling remains of windows, Faversham was blatantly flirting with Mrs Gibson and the girls, using all too familiar quotations from *Romeo and Juliet*. The words slipped out before Juliet could stop herself.

'*Oh swear not by the moon, th' inconstant moon,*

That monthly changes in her circled orb,

Lest thy love prove likewise variable.'

Faversham turned at the sound of her voice, his eyebrows raised sardonically. Mrs Gibson bristled, but Faversham spoke before she could intervene.

'*I pray thee, chide not: she whom I love now*

Doth grace for grace and love for love allow.'

Juliet could not overlook the sly glance he cast at Selina, who blushed prettily. If she had not spent so many hours reading and re-reading Shakespeare's play while she waited for Faversham to return, Juliet might not have recognised the quotation. But she too had plenty of obscure quotations stored up in her memory.

'Oh serpent heart, hid with a flowering face;

Did ever dragon keep so fair a cave?'

Faversham's eyes narrowed and his lips compressed. He stared at her hard, but Juliet refused to be cowed. She returned his stare and he was the first to blink. And then he began to clap his hands.

'Bravo, Mistress Governess. You really are as learned as Mrs Gibson says you are,' he said, with a palpable sneer in his voice as he turned back to the ladies.

Juliet shivered. She had seen something flicker across Faversham's face, as if it had suddenly struck him that he knew her from somewhere. Had she gone too far and put herself in danger? To add to her disquiet, she realised Amy was no longer by her side. Turning to look for her pupil, she caught Captain Gibson watching her with a speculative air. Had he overheard all or part of her verbal duel with Faversham?

They were picking their way across

the tussocky ground and last remaining flagstones towards the best-preserved part of the ruin, a tower which seemed to have been left almost intact. Amy had broken away from the rest of the group and was scampering on ahead. She darted through the dark, rectangular doorway at the foot of the tower.

'Amy, be careful,' Juliet cried out.

Amy's head popped around the edge of the doorway.

'Oh, do come and look. The staircase is still there and it looks quite sound.'

Juliet lengthened her stride, but she had too much ground to make up. Before she had reached the door, Selina, Faversham and the others had already packed inside the small, dark, circular chamber. Their voices echoed.

'The view must be magnificent from the top,' Faversham was saying.

'Amy, Selina, come down at once. It doesn't look safe,' Mrs Gibson called.

'Oh, but Mamma . . . ' both girls chorused.

Now her eyes had adjusted to the

gloom, Juliet could see the girls had begun mounting the stairs. Selina came down in response to her mother's command, but Amy, always the more defiant of the two, stood her ground.

'If the young ladies are willing to trust me, I'd be more than ready to escort them.' Faversham turned to Mrs Gibson. 'And I daresay Captain Gibson would be willing to risk his neck too in such a cause.'

'Oh, I am not averse to risking my own neck, as you so charmingly put it,' the captain replied dryly, 'but risking those of my cousins and their friends is quite another matter. I'm sorry, Amy, but I agree with your mother. The tower was precarious enough when I was a boy and I would rather consult someone who lives locally before I put you in any danger.'

With murmurs of discontent the party trooped out into the sunshine again. As they strolled on, Juliet became aware that Faversham had drawn Selina and Catherine Tibbs aside. The three of them were speaking in low tones, their heads close together. Then the girls giggled and Selina struck Faversham playfully with her fan.

Juliet's heart lurched. In normal circumstances Selina was almost too serious for her age. She would never have dared to do that to anyone she did not know well. To add to Juliet's suspicions, Faversham suddenly glanced over his shoulder at Captain Gibson. The latter remained unaware of the look, preoccupied as he was with Mrs Gibson and Miss Halliday.

'Miss Radley, do come and look.'

Amy had clambered over to one of the high, narrow, pointed windows in the outer wall of the castle. Juliet followed her and duly admired the view of the river and surrounding country-side. She couldn't help being aware of the walls towering precariously above them. Here and there individual stones had crumbled away and moss and hardy tufts of vegetation had sprouted in the crevices.

Laughter tinkled from somewhere above her. For an absurd moment, Juliet thought of the ghosts of the former inhabitants of the castle. Then her eye was drawn by a fleeting movement at the slit window a third of the way up the tower.

'Oh, that's Selina's laugh,' Amy exclaimed. 'They've gone without us.'

'Amy, no!'

It was already too late. The girl was running headlong for the door of the tower. Juliet hesitated a second and darted a glance at the main party. No one seemed to be looking in her direction and, discarding the dignity of a lady, she snatched up two handfuls of petticoats and ran.

Her gown streamed out behind her. She had forgotten how much fun it was to run; it had been such a long time since she had been permitted to do so. But she soon found herself short of breath. Her heart strained against her stays. She dared not run too fast, for fear of twisting her ankle. Amy, far more accustomed to running, out-stripped her effortlessly. By the time Juliet stumbled into the sudden dark-ness of the tower, the hem of Amy's riding habit was just vanishing round the first twist of the spiral staircase.

'Amy, come down at once,' Juliet gasped, knowing that it was hopeless. If Amy could defy her mother, she could defy her governess, whom she regarded as a slightly annoying playmate rather than as a figure of authority.

Briefly Juliet considered going to fetch help, or simply hoping that Amy would catch up with Selina and the others. But in her heart of hearts, she knew she had no choice. Amy was her responsibility and fetching anyone else would take valuable time.

Juliet drew in a deep breath and began to mount the spiral staircase, holding her petticoats out of the way with her right hand, while trailing the left carefully along the wall for support. She had never been particularly fond of towers and this one felt extremely narrow even though she was not wearing a hoop.

Above her she could hear merry chatter and laughter, though the echoes distorted the sound too much to be able to make out any words. She could see a shaft of light ahead from one of the slit windows and she forced herself towards it.

Footsteps echoed beneath.

'Miss Radley?'

Captain Gibson's voice made her start. She turned back as far as she could, her back against the outer wall.

'Yes?'

More steps as the officer clambered up the stairs into sight. 'What are you doing here? Didn't you hear us calling?'

'No, I — ' Perhaps she had been aware of distant voices while she was running, but there hadn't been time to pay heed to them. She changed tack. 'Amy dashed off after her sister and the others, and I thought I ought to fetch her back if I could.'

'Selina's here too?'

Juliet nodded. 'And Mr Faversham and Miss Catherine Tibbs, I think. At least, they were all together when I last saw them, and then Amy and I heard laughter from the tower.'

As if to confirm her story, voices drifted down the staircase.

'Well, I suppose there's no time to be lost. We'd better go after them.'

Juliet would far rather have gone down and left Captain Gibson to deal with the miscreants, but the spiral staircase was too narrow to allow her to squeeze past him comfortably. Taking a firm grip on herself, she forced herself to resume climbing.

It would have been dangerous to hurry. The steps were worn in places and narrower at one end than the other. The light fluctuated from gloom to sudden bursts of brightness from the slit windows. Juliet knew she had to pace herself carefully. She had no idea how high the tower was and did not want to exhaust herself long before she reached the top.

She couldn't help being conscious of Captain Gibson, carefully keeping a step or two behind her to avoid treading on her hem. It was reassuring to know he was there to catch her if she should trip. But she could also sense his displeasure that his advice had been ignored.

With every step she took, Juliet began to feel worse. Perhaps it was only her imagination, but the walls around her did not feel quite as solid as they ought to have been. Darkness hemmed her in.

She could not think at first what this reminded her of, though she felt she had once before been in this situation. And then she remembered.

Suddenly the voices became much closer, the light stronger, steadier. She picked out exclamations of wonder and excitement.

'Oh, look, there they are. Don't they look tiny?'

A few more steps and a doorway came into sight. Juliet's thigh muscles were aching from the climb. At least it was a room and not a flat roof at the top, she consoled herself. Then she stopped a few steps inside the room.

She was bathed in sunlight. The chamber was roofless, but what made Juliet's stomach churn was that one of the walls had crumbled away to waist height, leaving the room open to every wind. Amy was standing right on the brink, while the other three flitted from window to window, admiring the view.

'Amy,' she said in a low tone, terrified of startling the girl, 'come away from there.'

'Oh, Miss Radley. And Cousin Richard, too.' Amy's face blossomed. 'Isn't this fun?'

Juliet glanced at her companion. She saw his mouth twitch slightly, as if he was trying hard not to respond to Amy's enthusiastic greeting.

'Glad you decided to join us,' Faversham drawled, 'but as you can see, the young ladies are perfectly safe with me.'

'That's a matter of opinion,' Captain

Gibson replied curtly.

Their words began to merge into the background to Juliet. Insidious little voices were whispering in her head. *You might as well jump. You're going to fall anyway.*

The panorama that entranced the others made her dizzy. The tower seemed to sway with every gust of the breeze, which was sharper, stronger at this altitude than it had been on the ground.

Juliet dug her nails firmly into her palms. The others must never find out. She could hear Faversham and Captain Gibson exchanging sharp words, the three girls making excuses, taking the blame for the escapade, urging the captain to admire the scenery. He controlled himself with a visible effort so as not to spoil the girls' enjoyment, but Juliet saw him throw a dark look at Faversham.

'Do come and look, Miss Radley,' Amy urged. 'You can see all the way to Wales and there's the sweetest little mill a bit further upriver.'

Juliet forced herself to cross the heaving floor, though she felt as if she was wading through water. Her mind told her that the view was stunning, but she could not feel it in her heart. Not while dizziness and fear had her in its grip.

'It's — beautiful,' she said, 'but I rather think we ought to be going.'

As she turned away from the window, she came face to face with Captain Gibson. He gave her one aspiring look and before she knew how it had happened, her hand had been tucked through the crook of his elbow.

'Miss Radley is right,' he said. 'It would be selfish of us to keep the others waiting much longer.'

Juliet allowed herself to close her eyes for a second. Captain Gibson felt reassuringly steady and large beside her.

'Goodness, Miss Radley, how pale you look,' Selina exclaimed.

Juliet managed a smile as she opened

her eyes. 'It's nothing. I just don't have a very good head for heights.'

Faversham's gaze lingered a fraction too long on Juliet's face. For a moment he seemed to be groping for a memory. But just before she tore her gaze away from his, Juliet saw a spark of recognition in his eyes.

5

The descent was almost worse than the ascent. Faversham went first, to break the fall if anyone tripped, and then the girls followed, Juliet was not quite sure in what order. All she knew was that Captain Gibson insisted on taking her into his special care, going down immediately ahead of her so he could glance back at her from time to time and reassure himself that she had not fallen behind or fainted.

She told herself that with every step she was getting closer to the ground. From every window the view was becoming less vertiginous. Nearly there, nearly there. And yet she couldn't help thinking of that look Faversham had given her. Did he remember too?

She had met him one day in the graveyard next to the parsonage. A sudden shower had sent them scuttling for shelter in the little church. When the door opened two minutes later to admit someone else, Faversham had whispered 'come on' and dragged her through the heavy oak door into the bell tower. It had felt wildly sacrilegious and dizzyingly exciting, as he had pulled her up the staircase behind him.

At first she had giggled breathlessly, before the fear set in. But she had gone on nonetheless, determined to prove to herself that she could do it and nothing and nobody could harm her as long as she was with the man she loved.

The belfry had been frightening enough, but Faversham was not content to stay there. He climbed the ladder on to the flat roof. It had stopped raining by then, but the roof was slippery. Faversham hadn't even noticed she was afraid at first.

She ought to have guessed then that he did not really care about her feelings. He teased her and deliberately frightened her by leaning perilously far over the parapet. It had taken a burst of temper to persuade him to take her seriously and she had retreated precipitately inside and edged round the bells before he caught up with her.

Of course he had apologised and she had burst into tears as a reaction to the fright. She remembered snuggling against his breast, his arms wrapped tight around her, while he cooed soothing words in her ear.

Juliet shivered at the sound of Faversham's voice. He was helping Selena down the last few steps. Catherine Tibbs was standing on the threshold and Amy had apparently already raced off to find the others. Sensing Juliet's gaze, Faversham looked at her in the face. His eyebrows rose and his lips twisted in an ironical little smile.

'I take it I can leave the governess to your care, Gibson,' he drawled with the slightest hint of a sneer.

'With pleasure,' the other man replied.

Faversham offered one arm to each

of the girls as they emerged into the sunshine. Once again Juliet found Captain Gibson had tucked her hand through his arm.

'Thank you,' she said. She had not realised quite how shaken she was till now. A tremor had seized her whole body and her head was still light and dizzy.

'You'd better sit down,' he said, guiding her towards a broken segment of wall. 'Try to get a little colour back.'

Juliet smiled up at him unsteadily, but there was no time for her to reply.

'Well, Miss Radley,' Mrs Gibson demanded in her iciest tones, 'what do you mean by permitting my daughters to do something I had expressly forbidden?'

'I didn't . . . ' Juliet began faintly, but a large, firm hand gripped her shoulder and forced her down on to the wall.

'I think you'll find Miss Radley went to stop the girls, rather than encourage them.' Captain Gibson interposed himself between Juliet and her accuser.

'Now, do you have any hartshorn?'

Henrietta Gibson opened and closed her mouth like a fish, but instinctively fumbled in her pocket for her vial of smelling salts.

'Don't be cross, Mamma.' Amy tugged on her arm. 'It's my fault for running away when I promised Miss Radley I'd be good.'

'No, it's my fault,' Selina intervened. 'I wanted to see the view and Mr Faversham said he'd take us . . .'

'Something I had no business to do,' Faversham added. 'But I did so want to please the young ladies and I didn't see what harm it would do . . .'

Once again, their voices blurred around Juliet. All she was aware of was the pungent whiff of ammonia. She pushed the vial aside and a spark seemed to dart through her fingertips as she touched Captain Gibson's hand.

'Please don't make a fuss. I am quite recovered now,' she murmured.

Grave, grey eyes looked deep into hers and the words faded on her lips.

Then Captain Gibson straightened up.

'I think we've had enough self-recrimination for now,' he said. 'Isn't it time to be thinking about getting home?'

The whole party began to move back towards the waiting horses and landau. Juliet rose carefully. Her head was clearer and the shaking had stopped. She followed the others, keeping Amy in sight. But in the general bustle around the horses, Mrs Gibson drew her aside.

'Just remember this, Miss Radley. You may have deceived my cousin with your affectations of sensibility, but you cannot fool me. I shall be watching you like a hawk.'

★   ★   ★

By the time Richard had helped Miss Halliday mount her horse, Miss Radley had resumed her place on the box unaided. Richard found his eyes resting on the governess for a moment before he turned aside to fit his foot into his stirrup and haul himself up into the saddle. He could not help admiring her for her behaviour on top of the tower.

Faversham's horse passed close by the landau. Richard saw the other man turn and stare hard at the governess. She flinched barely visibly and dropped her head, pretending to brush a speck of dust from her gown.

Richard frowned. Juliet Radley had been much in his mind over the past weeks. He had come to look forward to their snatched conversations and until a week ago, he had thought the feeling mutual. Since she was closer to his age than any of the other young ladies at Winfield Hall, he found he had more in common with her.

But there was no escaping the fact that she had changed since Faversham's arrival. Every minute of that first night was etched on Richard's memory — her distracted air, her long silences, the way her eyes kept drifting towards that man.

At first he had thought there could be only one explanation — that Faversham's good looks had dazzled her, as they had virtually every other female at Winfield Hall, including the servants. But that did not explain the governess's reaction to Faversham's flirtation with the girls among the ruins. Generally Juliet Radley remained as unobtrusive as possible. It was wholly out of character for her to challenge Faversham in the way she had.

Could it be that Juliet had some prior knowledge of Faversham or his reputation? There seemed to be a suppressed antagonism between them. Initially, Juliet seemed to have had the upper hand. Now, though, the balance of power had shifted and Richard could not help feeling anxious for the governess' sake. If Faversham knew something to her detriment, he would not be scrupulous about using it. And Richard knew better than most how tenuous Juliet Radley's position was at Winfield Hall.

It was not that Henrietta never spoke of anything else, but when she did refer to the governess, it was with a mixture of mockery and irritation. Her complaints were always somewhat nebulous.

'It'll never come to any good.'

The words startled Richard out of his reverie. Colonel Halliday had drawn his horse alongside his, but the older man was staring at someone or something ahead of them.

'I don't know why the Gibsons permit it,' the colonel added with a shake of his unpowdered grey head. 'Wouldn't allow a scoundrel like Faversham anywhere near my daughter if I could help it.'

Alarm seized Richard. He had been gazing so intently at Juliet Radley that he had failed to notice Faversham had drawn his horse up alongside Selina's.

'A rake, is he?' he asked.

'Oh yes. Ruined and compromised several respectable young ladies and who knows how many maidservants and shopgirls. They say the father of one heiress paid him a large sum of money to break off the connection with his daughter. Not that the money stayed in Faversham's pockets for long.'

'It never does with that sort of man,' Richard agreed. He had seen a good deal of gambling and libertinism among his fellow officers and knew where it could lead. 'Have you spoken to my cousins yet?'

'For all the good it did me. Mr Gibson refuses to believe his daughter is no longer a little girl and therefore easy prey to an unscrupulous fortune hunter. And Mrs Gibson — well, she's inclined to think the tales about Faversham are exaggerated and therefore should be ignored.'

Richard could imagine Henrietta's irritable blustering. He had witnessed for himself how charmed she was when Faversham flattered and flirted with her. Richard doubted George had ever been so attentive, even when he was courting Henrietta.

'I'd better go, if you'll excuse,' Richard said. It was high time Faversham's tête-à-tête with Selina was interrupted.

The pair was so deeply immersed in conversation, neither of them heard him approach.

'A clergyman's daughter from Nottinghamshire, I believe,' Selina was saying. 'She told me once she became a governess because she has four or five younger brothers and sisters and the family needed money after her father died. Why do you ask?'

Faversham did not answer for a few seconds. Richard deliberately held back in the hopes of hearing his answer.

'I thought I recognised her, but could not place her at first. I believe I knew her many years ago, though she has changed a good deal since then, and not for the better.'

'Oh.' Selina squirmed uneasily. 'I think Miss Radley is quite pretty for a governess.'

'I agree,' Richard intervened, bringing his mount between theirs.

Selina started, but Faversham would not let anything discompose him.

'Ah, but you never saw Miss Radley in the first flush of youth. Such a shame that — well, never mind.'

'What's a shame?' Selina asked, though she had to crane forward to see past Richard.

'Um, oh — such a shame she never married,' Faversham replied, obviously changing what he had originally meant to say and cocking a beady eye at Richard to see if he would take the bait.

'It is, isn't it?' Selina agreed. 'I've always thought she would like a home of her own and a husband and children.' Her expression grew dreamy and Richard guessed it was not Miss Radley she was thinking about any more.

'But if that were the case, she would never have become your governess,' Richard pointed out quietly. 'And it's still not too late.'

Faversham smiled mysteriously, as if

he knew something they did not and Richard hastily changed the subject.

* * *

They passed a quiet evening, despite Faversham's best attempts to make the party as noisy as possible. The expedition must have exhausted everyone. Amy for once made no protest when Juliet suggested in an undertone that it was time to go to bed.

She had chosen her moment carefully, waiting until the others were too deeply immersed in their card games to notice them slipping away.

All evening Faversham had watched her. When she and Selina had played a duet on the piano, he had insisted on turning the pages for them. He had looked at her as if he wished to say something, but Selina's proximity made it impossible. Whatever it was that Faversham wanted to say to her, Juliet didn't want to hear it.

She didn't look back when she heard

a door opening softly behind her, just as she and Amy reached the first half-landing, where the stairs turned ninety degrees.

'Juliet.'

She turned instinctively, startled at hearing her own name, uttered by that voice of all voices. She was aware that Amy too had stopped dead, her eyes wide.

'Is that really your name?' she blurted out.

Juliet could not reply. Faversham had emerged from the shadows at the foot of the stairs and was staring at her intensely, smiling his most dangerous smile.

'I must speak with you, alone,' he said, completely ignoring Amy.

'I'm sorry. It's impossible. I have my duties to attend to . . . '

'I'm afraid I must insist,' he continued, still in a steady tone, not taking his eyes from her face. 'Or would you rather I spoke to Mrs Gibson?'

6

For two heartbeats, Juliet remained totally still and silent. Then Amy began to speak.

'What is it? What's wrong? Why do you need to speak to Mam — ?'

'Amy, go upstairs,' Juliet said, offering the candle to her pupil. 'I'll be with you presently.'

'Oh, but Miss Radley — '

'For once, Amy, do as you are told.'

The girl ruffled up and snatched the candlestick out of the governess's hand so violently that the flame flickered and molten wax ran down the candles. Faversham was leaning on the banister, watching them with an amused smile, as if it was a performance staged solely for his benefit.

Juliet waited till Amy had flounced away. She knew her pupil would make her pay for this scene, perhaps threaten to tell her mother what little she knew. But it couldn't be helped. She would have to find a way round it later.

As Amy retreated, Juliet felt welcoming shadows embrace her. Somehow she felt safer when Faversham could not see her expression. But she knew she had to go closer if she did not want anyone to overhear their conversation. Slowly she descended four or five steps, not quite to the bottom of the staircase, so she still had an advantage in height over Hugh Faversham and could keep the banister between them as a barrier.

'Well, well, fair Juliet,' he said. 'So it really is you. I didn't recognise you at first, you have improved so much since you were a gawky schoolgirl.'

Juliet smiled coldly.

'How strange,' she said. 'You never gave me the impression you thought me gawky at the time. And now I see you are pursuing a girl even younger than I was then.'

'Ah, you are angry with me and I cannot blame you.' Faversham dropped his voice and his expression softened. 'I admit I treated you shamefully. But have you ever considered I was not much more than an overgrown schoolboy myself at the time.'

'And what excuse do you have for your current behaviour?' she asked icily.

'If you mean my little flirtation with Selina, trust me, I mean no harm.'

'Trust you? You forget I know you better than anyone else in this house.'

Faversham bowed his head in mock-humility. 'I deserve your reproaches,' he said. 'Though if you remember, I did warn you I was a sad rake and you would do better to steer clear of me.'

'You know perfectly well that you didn't expect me to take you at your word. I daresay you have warned Selina about the same thing in exactly the same words.'

Faversham flinched and Juliet was startled to realise the blow had hit home. Not that he would let that hamper him. The tender expression vanished from his face. He leaned his elbow on the banister and rested his chin on his fist.

'I'd far rather be friends with you than otherwise, Juliet,' he said. 'But if you force me, I will go to Mrs Gibson and tell her what manner of woman is responsible for the morals of her precious daughters.'

'You wouldn't dare.' Surely it would harm his reputation too?

Faversham smiled and Juliet couldn't help thinking he looked like a cat toying with its prey.

'Wouldn't I?' he replied lightly touching her cheek with his fingertips as she flinched away.

At exactly the same moment, there was a surge of sound and Juliet found herself caught in a shaft of light from the open drawing room door. The silhouette of a man stood in the doorway. She turned away too suddenly to be able to identify him with any certainty. But she had the uneasy feeling it was Captain Richard Gibson.

★ ★ ★

It seemed a pity to waste such a glorious afternoon and so after dinner, the entire party set out for a stroll about the gardens. As it was Sunday, Juliet and Amy had been permitted to dine with the others and therefore were included in the party.

Inevitably Juliet brought up the rear, alone. Even Amy had deserted her, to chatter to her sister and the other girls, or to hang on Captain Gibson's arm and demand his attention, much to her mother's chagrin, as she was clearly trying to engineer a match between the Captain and Miss Halliday.

Juliet knew she was still not entirely in her pupil's good books, though Amy was never prone to hold a grudge for long. It had been no easy matter persuading her to go to bed the previous night. By the time Juliet reached the attic rooms, Amy was more bright-eyed than ever and agog with curiosity. Instead of getting undressed,

113

she had tried coaxing, promises of absolute secrecy, wild guesses and persistent questioning to try to extract the truth from her governess.

'Amy, please, go to bed. I'm tired and have a headache,' Juliet said at last, hoping to appeal to her pupil's better nature.

Amy threw an impudent glance at the governess before remarking casually, 'I wonder what Mamma would say if she knew you were meeting gentlemen in secret.'

The chill entered Juliet's soul, but she replied very quietly and steadily, 'More than likely she would have me sent away as a morally corrupting influence on you and your sister. Is that really what you want?'

Her tone seemed to shake Amy at last. 'Oh, but — she wouldn't do that. Not if I told her it was all Mr Faversham's fault . . . ' she stammered.

'Yes, she would. One thing you will learn is that in matters of morality, it is always the woman whose reputation suffers, even if she is an innocent victim.'

'Oh, but — but that's unfair!'

'Life is unfair and there's nothing anyone can do about it.'

Amy looked unconvinced, but she had finally submitted to get ready for bed.

As they trailed through the gardens, the party began to separate into smaller groups. Juliet followed at a slight distance. Amy was clinging to Captain Gibson's arm again, but after the scene on the staircase, Juliet was wary of approaching him.

He had not seemed his usual friendly self that morning when she and Amy joined the others before setting out for church. Instead he had scrutinised her closely and his bow seemed more aloof than in recent days.

The memory made her glance round. Selina and Faversham were both part of a large, noisy group of young people leading the way to the rose garden. Selina looked as if she was enjoying herself and Juliet judged she would be safe enough amid the crowd.

The scent of roses embraced her as she passed the gateway in the high hedge. Juliet leaned forward to caress one of the soft new buds, just opening to the bright day. She could hear Amy and Captain Gibson bickering amiably nearby.

'You agree with me, don't you, Juliet?'

It took her a moment to realise why Amy was smiling at her so sweetly.

'I'm afraid I haven't been paying heed to your conversation,' she replied, just as sweetly, 'and I don't recall giving you permission to call me anything other than Miss Radley.'

'Oh, but what's in a name?' Amy clasped her hands theatrically to her breast and rolled her eyes. 'That which we call a rose, by any other name would smell as sweet.'

Juliet shook her head, suppressing a laugh, though she couldn't help smiling. She knew she ought to put Amy in her place, but couldn't think how.

'I'm glad you've been acquainting yourself with the beauties of Shakespeare,' Richard Gibson replied dryly, but he caught Juliet's eye and she saw his cheek muscle twitch in an effort not to laugh. 'Perhaps you ought to make an intensive study of all his other plays as well.'

Amy shuddered expressively, covering her ears with both hands.

'If you make me do that, I'll run away from home,' she declared. 'How is anyone supposed to understand all those long words and odd sentences?'

Captain Gibson laughed, but then his expression grew darker, more speculative as he scanned Juliet's face. 'You forget, Amy, that Miss Radley is such a bluestocking, she seems to know half of *Romeo And Juliet* off by heart. I'm sure she'll be able to explain it to you.'

There was a sarcastic edge to his voice and Juliet was almost certain he was referring to the apparently clandestine meeting he had interrupted the previous night, as well as her confrontation with Faversham at the ruin. Perhaps he thought he had interrupted a lovers' tryst.

'Yes, well, girls are apt to do silly things when they are young and in love,' she said with a wry smile. 'Mine was to read and re-read that particular play. But I've discovered since that time that not all Romeos are as faithful as they profess to be.'

Too late Juliet realised Amy was listening to all this, wide-eyed.

'Selina said you'd had a tragic romance,' she said.

'Selina had no business telling you any such thing,' Juliet replied, blushing under Captain Gibson's grave look.

He seemed about to say something, but they were interrupted.

'Miss Radley.'

Juliet turned towards Mrs Gibson's voice.

'Yes, madam?'

'Will you kindly go and fetch Selina. There's something I must discuss with her.'

Juliet curtsied and obeyed. She suspected the errand had only been invented by Mrs Gibson to get the Captain away from the wholly unsuitable governess. But she was not entirely sorry to be sent away at this critical moment.

Richard watched Juliet Radley as she crossed the garden towards the party of young people in brightly-coloured coats or pastel-coloured gowns. He waited till he and Amy were alone before he asked with exaggerated casualness, 'So, how did you manage to guess Miss Radley's name?'

'Oh, I didn't guess,' Amy replied airily. 'Mr Faversham called her Juliet last night.'

Richard stiffened instantly. Hugh Faversham knew Juliet Radley's most closely guarded secret? So he had been right in deducing that Faversham's prior acquaintance with her went far deeper than he had admitted.

'When last night?'

'When I was going to bed. He came

after us into the hall and asked to speak to Miss Radley and she sent me off upstairs as if I was a baby.'

Clearly the same scene he had interrupted. He had not been absolutely sure the shadowy figure he saw was Juliet Radley, though he could not think who else it might be. He had left the drawing room after her departure because suddenly the triviality of the entertainment had annoyed him and he had thought a breath of fresh air might do him good. Instead he had ended up more perturbed than ever, not sure what he ought to believe.

Was that scoundrel trying to win Juliet back at the same time as he was courting Selina? There was no doubt in Richard's mind that Faversham had toyed with Juliet's affections in the past and he had met other men who could not be satisfied until every woman they knew was in love with them.

Surely Juliet was astute enough not to fall for the charms of a man who treated her with such pointed contempt and indifference in public, no matter what sweet words he lavished on her in private?

* * *

Juliet had managed to collect herself by the time she reached the merry little group. Then her steps wavered. Among all the beribboned hats and gauzy gowns, she could see no sign of Selina. She scanned the group again and her heart gave a tremendous lurch. Faversham was not there either.

A little further on, there was an opening in the high hedge, beyond which lay the kitchen garden — and the orchard. A sudden conviction struck her like a fist to the midriff.

They're in the orchard. They must be. They could not have left the garden by any other route without attracting attention. Visions of the parsonage garden came back to her and all that had happened there. Faversham kissing her, the scent of apples and new-mown grass . . .

She caught sight of the couple from a distance. They did not seem to see or hear her approach. Faversham's back was towards her and Selina only had eyes for him. The rustle of leaves masked the rustle of her petticoats. As Juliet hurried forward, Faversham laid a hand against Selina's still rounded, child-like cheek and tilted her face towards his.

'Selina!'

The cry was louder than Juliet intended it to be, sharp like that of a bird startled into taking flight. Selina started back, her cheeks crimson, but her eyes dazed, as if she had been woken in the midst of a beautiful dream.

'Ah, Miss Radley, what can we do for you?' Faversham asked with an insolent leer.

'For me, nothing. But Mrs Gibson wishes to speak to her daughter.'

She steeled herself to endure his

company as they returned to the rose garden. To her surprise, Faversham leaned coolly against the trunk of the nearest apple tree and allowed her to take Selina by the arm and lead her away.

They had not gone far, however, before Selina began to dawdle and cast imploring looks back over her shoulder. Juliet couldn't help wondering what game Faversahm was playing. Or did he really think she would not dare say anything to Selina?

'You really ought to be more careful of your reputation,' Juliet said in a low tone.

'Like you were, I suppose?'

Juliet stopped. She was not used to hearing that hard, sarcastic edge in Selina's voice. Fortunately they were no longer in sight of Faversham, though they had not quite reached the rose garden.

'What do you know about my past?'

'Everything. Hugh told me everything.'

Juliet felt the ground give way beneath her feet. Could it be — but no, there were things Faversham himself did not know and could not have discovered.

'He told me you were in love with him and made a fool of yourself.'

'What he did to me he'll do to you. Has he quoted Shakespeare or tricked you into kissing him by pretending he's got something in his eye?'

Selina whirled round. She had turned deadly white and Juliet knew she had struck a nerve.

'Have you been spying on me?' the girl gasped.

'No. Don't you see? He did exactly the same to me ten years ago.'

Selina pinched her lips together and moved on. She had pulled her arm free from Juliet's grip, but the governess still pursued her.

'You ask me why I'm not married, but shouldn't you also ask yourself why in all these years Faversham hasn't married either?'

She could not bring herself to utter the brutal truth to Selina's face, that Faversham had chosen her partly because she was so young and trusting, but also because her parents lived far away from the bustle of society and might not enquire too deeply into his character. Of if he did intend to marry her, it was almost certainly because he was on the brink of financial ruin.

'I only want what's best for you. I know how much you want to believe Faversham is in love with you. I know he makes you feel grown up and beloved. You are a beautiful, sweet-natured girl and one day you will meet a man who will adore you. Please don't ruin your chances, not for someone like Faversham.'

'You know nothing about him,' Selina was stung into replying.

'Don't you think if Faversham's intentions were honourable, he would have made a formal offer to your parents? Wouldn't he want to make sure you had enough pin money and were provided for in case you were left a widow?'

'Circumstances are difficult.'

'If he cannot afford to marry you, he ought to leave you alone.'

The mere thought made Selina cry out in pain.

'I have money, or I will, if Papa agrees.'

With that she flounced off to join her friends, leaving Juliet hesitating. She had no doubt that if Selina spoke to Faversham, he would be able to trump up some charge against her that Mrs Gibson would be only too pleased to believe.

7

'I beg your pardon, Miss Radley.' Captain Gibson's voice made Juliet spin round, her heart palpitating in her throat. 'I couldn't help overhearing the end of your conversation with Selina.'

Juliet realised he had just emerged from the shade of a nearby tree.

'How much did you hear?' she faltered.

'Enough to know you think she is in grave danger from a notorious libertine. I am right in thinking Hugh Faversham is the faithless Romeo you referred to earlier?'

Juliet hesitated, then nodded. Usually she would have not have interfered, but the situation was too serious to be swept under the carpet.

'I was only eighteen when he broke my heart,' she said simply. 'I can't stand by passively and watch him do the same to Selina. But Faversham has succeeded in turning her against me and nothing I can say will convince her.'

A shock ran through her as Richard Gibson placed his hand on her arm.

'You know you are not alone, don't you?' he said gently. 'I'm worried about Selina too.'

Juliet took a deep breath. 'So you'll speak to her parents? I'm afraid they may not take my fears seriously.'

'I'm not sure merely speaking to them will be enough. What we need is proof and I think I know where to find it.'

That same evening a long-faced Amy informed Juliet that her cousin had departed for a fleeting trip to Hereford and Bath, though he had promised to be back within the week. Having been brought up so far north that a journey to Bath took at least three days, it seemed inconceivable to Juliet that Captain Gibson's mission could be completed in so short a time and mentally she prepared for a far longer siege.

The days that followed were not easy ones for Juliet. Selina avoided her former governess as much as possible, not a difficult task since Juliet spent so much time apart from the rest of the family.

When Selina was upstairs, she was cool and distant, and since Amy was also present, private conversation was impossible. Besides which, Juliet could see that Richard Gibson was right. Merely talking to Selina would have no effect.

She soon realised she had made a terrible mistake in challenging Faversham about Selina. He obviously enjoyed parading the fact that the girl was so besotted with him, she hung on his every word, parroted his opinions, played the songs he professed were his favourites and dressed in her prettiest gowns just to elicit a word of praise from him.

As the days passed, Juliet saw with alarm that Faversham had begun the next phase of his campaign. At times he would seem his usual cheerful self and flirt with every lady within earshot, before he lapsed without warning into brooding melancholy. He started avoiding Selina, and then would gaze soulfully at her across the width of the room.

If Selina began to look hurt at his neglect, however, he would take a seat beside her and whisper something in her ear that would bring the dazzling smile back to her face.

Juliet tried in vain to persuade her former pupil that no man who truly loved her would torture her in this way, when he could just as easily go to her parents and ask for permission to marry her, but Selina would cover her ears with both hands.

Juliet lived in terror that Faversham would persuade Selina to elope with him or otherwise compromise herself before Captain Gibson returned. Nights were the hardest. Juliet lay awake for hours and the slightest noise could rouse her. She was terrified Selina might slip out of her room after everyone was asleep to meet Faversham.

As a result, Juliet was permanently tired, her eyes sore and red. It was hard to concentrate on her work and manage Amy's more wilful moods. If only Captain Gibson would come back and take some of the responsibility from her shoulders.

The long week stuttered to an end. Juliet was disappointed but not surprised that Captain Gibson still had not returned by Sunday evening. She would have to remain on guard for at least one more night, though she was not sure how much more she could endure.

She did not notice the following day that she kept wandering to the schoolroom window to gaze out at the drive until Amy pointed it out to her.

'Anyone would think you were waiting for someone to arrive.'

'Nonsense.' Juliet blushed, despite her best efforts. 'Now, have you learnt those French phrases I set you?'

'It's not very easy to learn anything

when someone keeps wafting past you.'

Her temper sharpened by tiredness, Juliet was tempted to give Amy a harsh retort, but she bit her tongue. Her pupil was right. She must have been a distracting presence and putting Amy's back up would not help in the slightest. She made an impetuous decision.

'It looks as if the skies have cleared. Why don't you change your shoes and fetch your hat so we can go out for our walk now?'

Amy rolled her eyes in astonishment, but she made no comment, terrified perhaps that her governess would change her mind. Indeed, Juliet had never known Amy to be ready quite so quickly in all the years she had lived at Winfield Hall.

As ill luck would have it, they met Faversham even before they reached the outer door. He raised his eyebrows quizzically.

'A bit early for your walk, isn't it?' he remarked.

'Miss Radley thought it might rain

later,' Amy replied.

But Faversham was not looking at her. His eyes bored into Juliet's, as if he was trying to penetrate her innermost thoughts. He shrugged, turned on his heel and vanished into the drawing room.

It was Amy's suggestion that they should go along the driveway as far as the gatehouse and Juliet deluded herself that if she had been on her own, she might have chosen some other route. They went at a brisk pace because the rain had cooled the air. The hedgerows and pastures looked much brighter and more vigorous than before the wet spell and the breeze cleared some of the congestion in Juliet's overtired brain.

It was not till they were coming back, however, that her ear caught the sound she had half-consciously been listening for. The steady clop of hooves made her heart contract with unexpressed hope, though she feared she would be disappointed when she found out who it was. She pretended not to hear until

Amy glanced round.

'Cousin Richard!'

A heavy weight tumbled from Juliet's shoulders and she couldn't help smiling as she turned towards the newcomer. Richard Gibson dismounted so he could walk alongside the others. Amy instantly claimed his attention, but for a moment his eyes met Juliet's above her pupil's tousled head and he smiled reassuringly.

'I hope you had a pleasant and profitable journey, sir,' Juliet said quietly.

'Yes, thank you. I think I have everything I need now,' he replied.

That was as much private conversation as they could manage in Amy's presence. The sun burst out from behind a cloud just as they came within sight of the main entrance to the house. At almost the same moment, three figures emerged from beneath the portico. Juliet scarcely noticed who the others were. All she knew was that Hugh Faversham had caught sight of them. His expression changed.

While the others took turns in welcoming Captain Gibson back, Juliet urged the reluctant Amy that it was time they returned to the schoolroom. As she followed her pupil indoors, Juliet was obliged to pass very close by Faversham, who stood nearest to the entrance.

In a low tone, so none of the others would hear, he murmured, 'Ah, now the mystery of your early walk is explained.'

Juliet threw him an indignant look, but she had no opportunity to justify herself. Besides, why should she care if Faversham thought she had arranged to meet Richard Gibson?

Then she realised where the danger lay. Faversham might tell Mrs Gibson that Juliet was a fortune hunter trying to marry into her employer's family. In which case, her only hope was that Richard Gibson would forestall him with some revelations of his own.

* * *

135

It was Faversham's idea that they should celebrate the return of the sunshine the following morning by breakfasting in the summerhouse. By the time the rowdy meal was over, the grass had dried and the weather was perfect for games on the lawn that sloped down to the lake.

There was, naturally, no question of Juliet being asked to take part in the riotous game of blind man's buff, but she was content to sit on one of the benches nearby and enjoy the warmth of the sunshine.

She smiled as Amy was almost cornered against a large stone urn full of summer flowers by the blindfolded Mr Parry. At the very last minute, Captain Gibson flew to her rescue. He hoisted the girl a foot or two off the ground, to create the illusion that she was taller than she really was.

Mr Parry ran his fingers carefully across Amy's face and declared that it could only be Miss Cecilia Tibbs, which made Amy giggle infectiously.

Richard Gibson turned his head slightly and caught Juliet watching him. His smile warmed her even more than the sun.

Abashed, Juliet looked away. He had come to sit beside her as usual the previous evening, but there had been no opportunity for them to speak privately. As a result, Juliet still did not know what he had discovered about Faversham, or if he had had a chance to speak to his cousins.

'Did you see what Cousin Richard did?' Amy was suddenly by her side, giggling.

'Indeed I did. Most unfair of you both to trick poor Mr Parry like that,' Juliet replied with a smile.

'All's fair in love and blind man's buff,' Amy replied judiciously. 'Where's Mamma? I wanted to talk to her.'

She dashed off before Juliet could reply. She was not alone for long, however.

'I'm getting too old for these games,' Richard Gibson said with an exaggerated sigh. 'Would you have any objection if I sat down for a moment?'

'Of course not,' Juliet replied.

He launched straight into an account of the evidence he had gathered. The news was grave enough. It seemed Faversham had run up considerable debts in Hereford on the understanding that he was soon to marry Selina and therefore her parents would pay his bills. But the revelations from Bath were even more startling.

'I gather that the father of a young lady whose acquaintance he made during the London season is threatening to sue Faversham for breach of contract unless he marries his daughter.'

'Yet another life ruined, whether he marries her or not. How can men be so cruel?'

'Not every man is a betrayer,' he said, softening his voice.

'No, but once a false step has been made, it cannot be retrieved.' Even as she uttered the words, she was acutely aware that Richard Gibson was so close that if he had chosen to do so, he could have kissed her.

'You were lucky to escape his clutches when you did.'

Juliet could not bring herself to reply to that remark. Instead she changed the subject. 'Have you spoken to Selina's parents yet?'

Captain Gibson shook his head. 'I haven't had a suitable opportunity. Maybe Faversham suspects what I intend to do. At any rate, he has barely left Henrietta's side since I returned and without her to push him on, George will do nothing.'

Juliet dropped her head. He squeezed her hand, briefly but powerfully.

'Don't look so downcast. Henrietta is bound to act on incontrovertible proof that Selina's reputation is at risk. And as far as I can make out, Faversham was courting this other girl at exactly the same time that he started dancing attendance on my cousins — I doubt Selina will forgive his infidelity.'

'I hope you're right.'

Juliet allowed her eyes to drift across the merry throng of young people. A dart of ice pierced her as she met Faversham's gaze. How long had he been watching them?

The game of blind man's buff was descending into chaos. Pretty soon the ladies were subsiding on to the benches like swans on their nests, while the younger gentlemen sprawled on the grass at their feet. Fan after fan flicked open. All except Selina, who searched her pockets in vain.

'How provoking. I must have left it in the summerhouse,' she said. 'I'd better go and fetch it.'

'Why not allow me to go instead?' one of the gentlemen offered.

'No, no, don't desert us,' the oldest Miss Tibbs cooed, fluttering her lashes. 'Mr Faversham has already disappeared somewhere and we cannot spare another gentleman.' She tossed a supercilious look over her shoulder. 'The governess can go just as well. She's been doing nothing all morning.'

'I'd far rather do it myself,' Selina protested, but she was overruled by her mother.

Juliet did as she was bid, though it rankled that she had still not acquired a name as far as some of the guests were concerned. The only person who might have interceded on her behalf was Captain Gibson and he was too busy in fending off Amy's offer to crown him with a daisy chain she had just made.

It didn't take long for Juliet to reach the summerhouse, which was screened from the lakeside by a high hedge. It was an open-sided, circular building with a row of columns supporting the roof. She shivered as a sudden cloud obscured the sun.

Juliet swept up the three wide, marble steps and looked around. All the dishes and remaining food from breakfast had been removed and it struck her that the servants might have found Selina's fan and taken it with them to restore to its mistress later. However, she had better look around now she was here, even if she had to return empty-handed.

She took a few steps forward, searching for the glint of gilt edging beneath the benches and table.

'Looking for something?'

A masculine voice made Juliet spin round, her heart thudding against her stays. Faversham was lounging against one of the columns, watching her with an amused smile. He was holding Selina's fan, which he unfurled with a deft flick of the wrist.

It flashed across Juliet's mind that this was an assignation. No wonder Selina had been so eager to fetch the fan herself. Juliet had merely assumed the girl was unwilling to accept favours from her former governess because of their recent disagreement.

'Miss Gibson asked me to come and find her fan,' she replied.

'Did she, by jove? Or did you persuade her that it would be much better for her reputation if you came instead?'

Juliet flushed, but she would not admit that she had bent the truth.

'Please give me the fan. The others will be waiting for me.'

'Surely you are in no desperate hurry to return to your duties?'

Their eyes locked in a battle of wills. Faversham's dangerous smile only widened. He flicked the fan shut and put both hands behind his back.

'I'll tell you what, I'll let you have the fan if you can guess which hand I am holding it in.'

'I don't have time for these babyish games.'

'Tush, tush, Miss Radley, why so impatient?'

Juliet drew in a deep breath. She had to think clearly. Maybe there was some way of outwitting or persuading Faversham. Or perhaps she would have to wait until he tired of these silly games. But time was not on her side. The skies were darkening ominously and she knew that if she did not set out soon, she would never reach the others before the inevitable downpour.

'Very well. Have it your own way. I hope I can trust you to return the fan to Miss Gibson?' Juliet turned to leave, but Faversham barred her way.

'You cannot possibly go now. The shower will soon be over.'

She hesitated, weighing up the alternatives.

'Quite like old times, isn't it, Juliet?'

'Miss Radley to you, sir.'

'Oh, come now, we never used to be so formal.'

Her only reply was a look of pure contempt.

'Don't be cross with me, Juliet,' Faversham murmured, making puppy-dog eyes at her. 'You're much prettier when you smile.'

Juliet did not answer and dodged round one of the columns, only to find Faversham yet again blocking her way out.

'Do you never think of those times?' he persisted. 'I do — frequently. And then I start to wonder what other people would think if they knew. People like Mrs Gibson or the captain.'

Juliet's blood ran cold, though he spoke in his gentlest tones.

'What do you want from me, Faversham?'

'Isn't it obvious?'

Juliet shivered as he ran his fingers across her cheek.

'No,' she whispered.

'Not even to save your beloved pupil from my clutches?'

Before Juliet could react, Faversham had pushed her against the nearest column. One of his arms twined round her waist, while with the other hand he tilted her face back. His lips pressed insistently against hers.

Revulsion filled her. With both hands, she thrust against his chest, trying to push him away from her, but he only gripped her tighter, his fingers burrowing deep into her hair. Her neck ached from trying to turn her face away. His hot, wet, grasping mouth smothered her cries.

Even as she struggled against Faversham, Juliet became aware of noises, the throb of increasingly heavy rain on the roof, distant voices, then the patter of feet on the marble steps.

'Miss Radley! What is the meaning of this unseemly display?'

Juliet's heart leapt in terror at the sound of Mrs Gibson's voice. Faversham had loosened his hold on her and she pushed him away from her with all her force. But as she turned to face her mistress's wrath, fear closed her throat.

Mrs Gibson had not come alone. Among the cluster of figures, Juliet was vaguely aware of Selina's pale, stricken face. But her eyes were inevitably drawn to the tallest figure in the group and the expression in Richard Gibson's eyes made her heart quail.

8

'Well?' Mrs Gibson demanded. Juliet hadn't known it was possible to inject so much menace into a single syllable.

'It's — it's not my fault. He forced himself on me . . . '

Mrs Gibson sniffed disbelievingly. Her contemptuous look made Juliet suddenly aware that Faversham had pulled several pins from her hair and it was beginning to unravel and tumble down over her shoulders.

'Oh, come now, Juliet, there was hardly any need for force.'

Juliet turned on Faversham, rendered almost speechless by his effrontery. He was leaning against the nearest column, his arms folded, an amused half-smile on his lips.

She realised vaguely that she had expected him to do the honourable thing and take the blame on himself.

Instead he had evidently decided to brazen things out and did not care in the slightest that he would ruin her reputation in the process. Or perhaps that was precisely why he was behaving in this way.

'How can you tell such lies?' she demanded. 'Have you no sense of honour left?'

'Miss Radley, you forget yourself,' Mrs Gibson intervened coldly. 'I won't have you speaking in such a manner to any of my guests.'

Juliet was left groping for words, stung by the injustice. What was she to do if she was not even allowed to defend herself?

'You are unfair, Henrietta. Surely Miss Radley has as much right to defend herself against Faversham's slurs as any other member of this household?'

Incredulously, Juliet looked up. Captain Gibson had separated himself from the rest of the group to interpose himself between her and Faversham.

'I should have thought it was perfectly obvious what is going on,' he went on. 'Not content with trying to seduce your oldest daughter, that villain is attempting to do the same to her governess.'

Juliet heard Selina utter a pained cry.

'Is that what you really think, Gibson?' Faversham drawled. 'Or are you simply jealous that Juliet prefers my company to yours?'

Fear leapt into Juliet's throat. Everyone present must have known exactly what he was insinuating about her character.

'Beware of how you slander Miss Radley's good name,' Captain Gibson growled.

But Faversham merely laughed. 'Brave, Juliet,' he purred. 'I see you've found a gallant champion at last, eh? But the question is — would he be so willing to defend you if he knew you as well as I do?'

Everything happened too fast. One moment Faversham was watching the scene with a smug smile. The next, Richard Gibson had leapt forward and felled him with a single blow. Juliet found herself buffeted to one side by the sudden surge as they crowded forward to help Faversham to his feet and keep both combatants apart.

'I've called men out for less than that,' Faversham panted as he hauled himself up. His eyes gleamed dangerously as he looked at Juliet and the Captain.

'I'll give you satisfaction any time you choose,' Captain Gibson flashed back, despite the cries of horror from the spectators.

Terror filled Juliet's heart. The thought of Richard Gibson risking his life in a duel was more than she could bear.

'No,' she cried out, grasping his arm with both hands. He was panting heavily and she had never seen him look so angry. 'Please, please, sir, don't do this.'

On top of everything else, she knew

she would be ruined if she were believed to be the cause of a duel. It would be assumed that only improper behaviour on her part could have provoked the men to such a pitch.

Juliet's appeal obviously made Captain Gibson waver. But it was not for him to withdraw the challenge since he had not issued it. Nor would he offer the apology, which, Juliet knew, was the only gentlemanly way out of this situation. Everything depended on Faversham, who seemed to be enjoying her discomfiture far too much to draw back now.

'You'd be well advised to take Juliet's advice,' he drawled. 'Her reputation is not worth your life, or mine.'

'She's worth ten of you, and I'd die willingly in her defence.'

Faversham raised his eyebrows. 'And suppose I told you about a long, hot summer we spent together many years ago?'

A bitter smile crossed Richard's face. 'I hardly think it would be much to your credit to expose how you broke the heart of an innocent girl.'

'Is that what she told you? There's a little more to the tale than that.'

Juliet felt the ground give way beneath her feet. The thing she had feared most had finally happened. This was the end of her career as a governess. But worse, far worse would be for Richard Gibson to find out about her past in this way. She would almost have preferred it if Faversham had shouted his revelations from the rooftop to the assembled household.

'No one is interested in your lies,' Richard retorted, but Henrietta intervened.

'On the contrary, I would be most interested to hear what Mr Faversham has to say.'

Juliet felt as dizzy as if she was suffering from a high fever. All around her she could sense the others watching, agog with curiosity. Even Amy had been stunned into silence.

'What shall I tell her, Juliet?'

Faversham cocked an impudent eye at the governess. 'About our long walks along country lanes? About the church tower? About how you used to climb out of windows to meet me in your father's orchard? Wouldn't you have done anything to please me then?'

For the first time in a long while Juliet lost her temper. Faversham had pushed her too far. Before she had time to think, she had struck him across the face with all her might. She heard gasps all around her, as she backed off, horrified at what she had done. An angry red mark flared on Faversham's cheek.

'You see, Gibson, I've no need for lies. Doesn't her behaviour suggest she has something to hide?'

'That's enough,' Mrs Gibson thundered. 'I won't have such scenes in my home. You may go and pack your bags, Miss Radley. And you need not expect me to give you a letter of recommendation, not after all I have witnessed.'

For a moment Juliet was paralysed,

stunned by the speed of events. She scarcely heard Richard Gibson's protest. Then she turned abruptly on her heel and fled, unable to look into any of those accusing eyes any more. Only in passing she caught a glimpse of Selina and Amy's ashen faces.

★　★　★

The next hour passed in turmoil for Richard. He could not bring himself to regret defending Juliet or accepting Faversham's challenge, but he was in anguish that his loss of temper had led to Juliet's dismissal.

He had done his utmost to try to persuade Henrietta to change her mind, but she was adamant.

'You must understand, Cousin, that I have to take every precaution that the character of the woman responsible for my daughters' morals should be unimpeachable.'

'And so you would rather believe the slanders of a notorious rake?'

'Caesar's wife must be above suspicion,' Henrietta replied, sniffing pointedly.

Richard was tempted to point out that her flirtation with Faversham had not gone unnoticed, but this was not the right time to antagonise his cousin's wife any further.

He knew it would be worse than useless to try to persuade George to reverse his wife's decision. All his cousin would do was shrug his shoulders uneasily and murmur that he always left such matters to Henrietta.

His way was clear now. There was only one more thing he could do to save Juliet's reputation. His only qualms were on her account, in case she did not return his feelings.

Almost by instinct he made his way up the spiral staircase. Muted sounds came from the nearest room, the swish and thud of drawers being opened and closed, the whisper of linen or cotton as it was folded, footsteps across the bare floorboards. But it was the murmur of Juliet's voice that propelled him through the door without even a preliminary knock.

Two women were just closing the lid of a modest trunk. Henrietta had clearly sent a maid to assist Juliet to speed the process of packing, or perhaps to make sure the governess did not steal anything.

Both women rose at the sight of him. Every drop of colour had drained from Juliet's face, but she seemed oddly, dangerously calm, as if she was barely keeping a torrent of emotion in check. Only her eyes gazed at him intently, pleadingly.

'I'm so sorry that it should have come to this, Miss Radley,' There was such a lot Richard wanted to say to her, but the presence of the servant deterred him.

Juliet dismissed his words with a shrug. 'It's not your fault.'

'Of course it's my fault. Perhaps if I spoke to my cousins one last time . . .'

'It won't do any good. Mrs Gibson has been determined to get rid of me for a good while. Nothing you can say will make any difference.'

He heard the hardness of suppressed tears in her voice as she turned her head aside.

'Where will you go?'

'My mother is staying with one of my brothers at present. He's a tenant farmer some miles north of Nottingham. They haven't much room, but I hope I'll be able to make myself useful until I find somewhere else to stay.'

There was silence for a moment, while the maid finished fastening the trunk. Richard struggled for words, but in the event it was Juliet who spoke first.

'I hope, sir, you'll say goodbye to the girls for me and tell them I shall miss them.'

'Henrietta forbids you to say goodbye?'

Juliet bit her lips and nodded jerkily.

'They'll be sorry they didn't have the opportunity to say farewell.'

She turned abruptly towards the

mirror to fasten the ribbons of her broad-brimmed hat. Richard caught a glimpse of her reflection. Her eyes were so clouded; he suspected that everything she saw was blurred.

He was on the verge of saying something impetuous, despite the presence of the maid, but at exactly the same moment someone tapped at the door.

'The carriage is ready, miss,' the footman announced.

'Thank you. Perhaps you'd be good enough to carry my trunk down for me?'

This was his last opportunity, Richard thought. If he didn't speak now, he might never see her again and he knew he could not bear for that to happen.

'Miss Radley.' Juliet started at the sudden desperation in his tone, but he went on regardless. 'Before you go, I must speak to you in private.'

For a moment Richard thought she was going to refuse.

'Very well,' she said quietly. 'Perhaps

we could go to the schoolroom. I must check I have left nothing behind.'

Like a forlorn dog sensing that his master would be leaving him, Richard trailed after her along the short passage. He had never realised till now quite how unbearable life would be at Winfield Hall if he was deprived of the hope of seeing Juliet or exchanging a few words with her. He had not intended to speak to her so soon of such things, but circumstances had forced his hand.

Her eyes were feverishly bright as she turned towards him.

'Juliet . . . ' he began, but to his surprise she clutched his arm with both hands.

'Please, sir, whatever you do, don't fight this duel with Faversham.'

Her closeness made him catch his breath.

'I don't see how I can withdraw with any honour,' he replied slowly, to give himself time to think. 'But since Faversham was the one to issue the challenge, he will be seen as the aggressor and I will be able to set my own terms. I swear I shall do my utmost to prevent loss of life on either side. I'll even accept concessions if Faversham's second offers any.'

She shook her head. He could see the torment in her eyes. Unconsciously, she clung even more tightly to his arm.

'Please, for my sake, give it up. I couldn't bear it if anything happened to you and I knew it was all my fault. Hasn't that man ruined enough lives already, without adding yours to the number?'

Her tone made his heart beat faster. Perhaps — was there a chance that she was so distressed because she cared for him? He softened his voice.

'For your sake I would do a good deal.' He could not resist the temptation to stroke her cheek and she flushed under his touch. 'But don't you see it is for your sake that I am bound to do this, to clear your name?'

Her face contorted in agony. She

lifted both hands to her temples and shook her head again. 'No, no, that is the worst possible reason to fight this duel. Faversham was right — I am not worth the tiniest drop of your blood.'

'I don't agree. You are a good and kind person and don't deserve to have your name besmirched in this way.'

Juliet managed a tremulous smile. 'Ah, you don't know me at all,' she said. 'And this duel will only add fuel to the speculation about the extent of my acquaintance with Faversham. Is that really what you want?'

Richard hesitated. He knew she was right, at least to a degree. 'Nothing can stop gossips from talking,' he replied gently, 'but if we were to be married . . . '

He never finished his sentence. Juliet's head shot up, her eyes wide, as if she could not believe what she had just heard.

'No,' she whispered. 'No, I mustn't listen to this.'

She pushed past him to the door. But

Richard could not let her go so easily.

'I love you, Juliet. Won't you give me the right to protect you?'

His words stopped her in her tracks. She turned towards him, her lips parted as if she wanted to say something, and her eyes raked his face.

'I know I've nothing to offer you, apart from the pittance of my half-pay,' he stumbled on, 'but — but I want to marry you, if you will have me.'

He thought he could see desperate longing in her eyes, but something about her frozen pose prevented him from stepping closer and taking her into his arms. She swallowed.

'You don't know what you are asking.'

'Would it be so hard? I thought — was it just my imagination? I thought you were — at least fond of me.'

'Don't tempt me, please, please.'

He wanted to respect her wishes, but the tone of her voice betrayed her. She did care for him. He reached out for her, but she whisked away towards the stairs. There she made the mistake of looking back. Her eyes filled with tears and as she plunged down the staircase, he followed her, not caring who might see them.

He caught up with her in the entrance hall. Through the window, the carriage was visible, waiting on the gravel driveway, her meagre possessions already hauled on to its roof. But apart from the servants outside, there was nobody about.

'Miss Radley — Juliet, we cannot leave things like this. Won't you at least say goodbye?'

She turned slowly towards him. 'Goodbye, Captain Gibson.'

Unwillingly she raised her eyes to his face and then seemed unable to look away. Without any conscious thought, Richard found himself drawn towards her. He cradled her cheek in his hand and tilted her lips towards his so he could kiss her, desperately, hungrily.

For a long, exquisite moment, she

yielded to him. Then she ripped herself away, gasping the single word.

'No.'

As she pushed her way through the door, he followed her out on to the driveway.

'I'm sorry. I didn't mean to take advantage of you like that.' Was there anything he could say to make her change her mind? Or had he behaved too much like Faversham to earn her forgiveness? 'I swear to you I am nothing like Faversham. I'll never betray you, if you could bring yourself to trust me.'

She ducked her head, but Richard thought he caught the glimmer of tears in her eyes. 'You don't understand. I do trust you. But there are things about my past you do not know.'

She started moving towards the carriage, but Richard caught hold of her hand to detain her 'I forgive you, whatever you think you have done wrong. What can be so terrible that we cannot overcome it together?'

She looked up at him then. 'You really want to know?' she asked in a low, trembling voice. 'Everything Hugh Faversham said about me is true, and even he doesn't know the worst. He didn't merely toy with my affections. He seduced me in my father's orchard. I didn't know how to tell my parents, but my mother found out two months after he abandoned me when — when I miscarried his child.'

Stunned by the revelation, Richard staggered back. Images flashed before his eyes and suddenly he understood many hints that had almost escaped him before.

Before he could recover, Juliet had yanked her hand away from him and was clambering into the carriage. He forced himself to run after her, but as in a dream, his legs did not seem to work. The door slammed and he heard Juliet cry out 'drive on' to the coachman. He had the impression of large, haunted eyes gazing back at him from the window and his steps faltered as the carriage pulled away beyond his reach.

★ ★ ★

It's all over. It's all over, Juliet told herself. She had done the right thing. It was the only way to turn him against her. Now perhaps the duel could be averted. And Richard Gibson was an honourable man. He would not spread her shameful secret. Not that it mattered any more. She would never be able to go back, or even to correspond with her former pupils.

And yet, and yet . . . If she had done the right thing, why was she so miserable? Until now she had managed to keep herself in check, but now the need for immediate action was over, she seemed to give way all at once.

Her mind was flooded with images of Richard and what their future might have been if she had held her tongue. But no, it was better she had told him now. He would have found out the truth about her on their wedding night and then the outcome would have been more devastating.

I was right to do it. It is better this way. But oh, I never knew how much I loved him till now.

9

It was odd, Juliet thought. She had never realised how much secret hope she still harboured in her heart until the last fragment of it was gone.

She had been staying at her brother's farmhouse for almost a month now, sharing a room with her mother because there was no other space available. Her unannounced arrival had caused consternation in the family, especially when she had been forced to reveal that she had been dismissed without a letter of recommendation. After all her years of hard work, all she had to show were her modest savings.

For the first few days, she had been capable of nothing. The slightest excuse was enough to reduce her to tears. She avoided company and had only gradually begun to help around the house.

Instead she scoured the newspapers

in the vain hope of some reference to the duel, even though it was not local nor of national importance. The worst torment was not knowing the outcome — whether George Gibson or Colonel Halliday or some other intermediary had been able to prevent it, or, if it had taken place, who had emerged the victor. Had one of the men been injured or killed and his opponent forced into exile or charged with murder or manslaughter? So many things could have gone wrong.

What if Richard Gibson was dead? Juliet shrank from the thought, and yet it pursued her. Night after night, she woke to feel his burning kiss upon her lips. His image haunted her.

But even in those miserable days, the sound of hooves or a man's voice in the yard had made her prick up her ears and it slowly dawned on her that, despite everything, she had secretly hoped that Richard Gibson would come after her, to tell her that her past made no difference to him, that he still loved her and wanted to marry her.

Now, on this painfully beautiful summer day, it was brought home to her that all her hopes were in vain. She had learned nothing in all the years since she had waited for Faversham to return and ask her parents for permission to marry her. Richard wasn't coming and she would have to start making new plans so she didn't become a burden on her family. The trouble was that as a lady, her choices were severely limited.

In the meanwhile, she could make herself useful by helping to harvest the soft fruits in the kitchen garden at the rear of the farmhouse.

The mechanical task suited Juliet. It gave her an occupation but left her free to think or to join in the chatter with her mother, sister-in-law, Annie, and six-year-old niece, Polly, who was also helping.

The latter even made Juliet smile when she patted her younger brother on the head and told him solemnly,

'You stay here and play. I've got work to do.'

But despite the merry chatter, in the stillness of the summer's afternoon, they all heard the creak of the gate and the thud of hooves.

'I'd better go and see who that is,' Anne said, ruefully licking her juice-stained fingers and trying to rub them clean against her apron as she hurried off.

Juliet suppressed the half-formed hope that still came to her instinctively and instead turned her attention to Polly, who was prattling excitedly about jams and preserves and pies and all the other good things that would be made of the fruit once it was ripe and picked.

Juliet didn't even notice when Anne returned to the kitchen garden. Nor had she come alone.

'Juliet, there's someone here to see you.'

She turned and momentarily she was dazzled by the pristine red coat, trimmed with gold braid and set off against the whiteness of the newcomer's waistcoat and breeches.

'Good day, Miss Radley.'

'Captain Gibson,' she gasped as her eyes flew upwards and were caught and held by an intense grey gaze. 'Thank God, you're alive.' She scanned him hastily for any sign of injury, a bandage or a sling. And yet her eyes were drawn irresistibly back to his face. 'You're not hurt?'

'No, not a scratch on me,' he replied, offering her his hand.

Juliet was ashamed of how hot her hand felt as he grasped it with his usual firmness. 'What about Faversham?'

'Nothing dented bar his pride. A mere scratch with the sword, half-healed already.'

Juliet let out a long breath as relief washed over her.

'Thank God,' she repeated in a whisper. She tore her gaze away from his face, afraid he would see the longing in her eyes, but she could still feel him watching her.

'I would have come sooner to relieve you of your anxiety, but legal and regimental business detained me,' Richard went on.

'I gather you managed to obtain a new commission?' she said. It only occurred to her then that he was still holding her hand, because she could not bring herself to withdraw it.

'I was fortunate that Colonel Halliday was willing to use his influence on my behalf,' he replied. 'It's a more senior regiment, less likely to be disbanded and all in all a much better prospect for future promotion than . . . ' He stopped himself, aware he was babbling merely to fill the silence.

'That's good news.' She managed to smile as she glanced up. And then at last their fingers slid apart, leaving Juliet feeling bereft.

She gathered enough wits to introduce him to her family, but all the while she was fighting not to ask the question that was on the tip of her tongue. Why are you here?

Richard declared himself delighted to meet everyone, then turned back to Juliet.

'Could I perhaps have a word with you in private, Miss Radley?' he suggested. 'I am the bearer of news and messages for you from Herefordshire.'

'From Amy?' Juliet asked, leading the way to the orchard adjoining the garden.

'And from Selina. They both sent you letters.'

As Richard fumbled in his pockets, Juliet took the opportunity while his head was bowed to run her eyes hungrily across his face. Her gaze lingered on his broad forehead, etched with its three faint furrows.

She noted the neatness of his ear, set close against the side of his head, the straightness of his nose, the faint suspicion of a shadow above his upper lip and along his jaw . . .

He looked up and she flinched at being caught out.

'I trust you left them all well,' she

said, but her voice was so faint, it seemed to come from beyond the next hill.

'Tolerably well. Amy misses you and she was annoyed she wasn't allowed to say goodbye.'

He offered her two carefully folded and sealed packets. A spark leapt from fingertip to fingertip as their hands touched. Juliet glanced down at Amy's untidy, childish scrawl and Selina's more sophisticated loops and hooks, but she made no attempt to break the seals just yet.

Instead she toyed with the letters as they strolled on, side by side, beneath the trees, which were laden with hard, green apples and pears.

'Amy told me you were not to mind if there are more spelling mistakes than usual in her letter because she was in a hurry and had a vast deal to say and no time to go back and correct herself. Oh, and she says the new governess is nowhere near as nice as you, but she is trying hard to be good, though it is so tempting to put a frog in her bed.'

Juliet laughed out loud. 'She's incorrigible.'

Richard smiled too. 'To be honest, I think she can't wait till she is old enough to do without governesses altogether.'

Smile met smile. Eyes locked and for a moment, time stood still.

'And Selina?'

Richard suddenly looked grave and Juliet's heart lurched in alarm.

'Well,' he said, slowly, 'you'll be pleased to hear she has not eloped with Faversham. In fact, I think all fears on that account are over. The most fortunate consequence of the duel was that it forced Faversham to leave Winfield Hall because, being related to me, George and Henrietta were obliged to take my side in the affair.'

'That's something to be grateful for.' Juliet allowed herself a wry smile. 'How is Selina bearing up?'

'As well as can be expected. The poor child was devastated at witnessing that little scene in the summerhouse. I found her in tears after you'd departed because Faversham had lied to her about his past acquaintance with you.'

Juliet glanced up at the change in his tone. He was gazing at the fields of ripening wheat beyond the fruit trees.

'There's something else, isn't there?' she challenged him.

Richard looked uncomfortable. 'I'm sorry. I didn't mean to do it initially, but I was obliged to tell Selina about your secret. It was the only way to prevent her from forgiving Faversham. I tried telling her at first about all the other girls he has betrayed, but a stranger's tale never has the same effect as the story of someone you are close to.'

'Oh.' Juliet's mind worked, trying to assimilate the idea and decide what she felt about it.

'Don't worry about Selina. I swore her to secrecy and she can see why she must not tell her sister or her parents.'

Juliet nodded. Selina always had been

dependable, even as a child. But still, the thought that her former pupil knew her secret made Juliet uncomfortable. Abruptly she turned away from her companion. The farmhouse was barely visible between the trees. She had not realised they had come such a long way.

'Perhaps we ought to turn back,' she began.

'Juliet.'

His voice was low, urgent, and for a moment she even doubted whether he had really uttered her name, or if she had merely imagined it. His fingers brushed against her sleeve and just as abruptly withdrew. Throughout their stroll, she had been tormented by how close he was to her and yet she was forbidden to reach out and touch him.

'I didn't come all this way merely to discuss my cousins, much as I love them,' he said. 'I — I've come to renew my suit.'

Had he really said what she thought he had said? His voice was so soft, so tender. She could feel her face glowing.

She wanted to believe this and yet . . .

'I won't lie to you. The life of a soldier's wife, even an officer's, is not an easy one. Money is not as plentiful as many suppose and you are perpetually moved from place to place. As for times of war . . . ' He shuddered. 'Having seen what I have seen, I had determined to remain a bachelor rather than expose the woman I love to such hardship and danger. And yet despite all this, I find I cannot bear to live without you.'

Juliet raised dazed eyes to his face. 'Are you sure you have thought this through properly?'

'I've thought of nothing else these past weeks. Don't you realise it was for your sake that I spent so much time obtaining this commission, so that I would have something to offer you as a husband?'

The temptation to give way was almost overwhelming. 'What about your family? Won't they object?'

'On the contrary, I'm certain Amy

will be delighted.'

'You know that's not what I meant. If they knew about my past . . . '

'But they don't, and what does it matter anyway?' He caught both her hands. 'You trusted an unprincipled villain when you were little more than a child and he betrayed you. He is the one who ought to be ashamed, not you. Doesn't everyone deserve a second chance?'

'Not many people would agree with you,' Juliet forced herself to say. 'That's why I'd made up my mind to stay a spinster and take care of my parents in their old age. But when Papa died, we needed money and so I had to work . . . '

Her voice trailed away at his grave look.

'I take it you have never been tempted to stray again?'

'No.'

'And how many people know of your — misfortune?'

'Only Mamma. She followed me to

my room when the pain began and she guessed. She took care of everything and wouldn't let the servants or the doctor into the room. She refused to tell Papa because she knew he would insist that Faversham should marry me and then it would all come out in the open. I half-hated Faversham by then for what he had done to me and Mamma said she would never consent to my marrying such a man . . .'

'She was right,' Richard said. 'Even if he could have been induced to do the honourable thing, Faversham would have broken his marriage vows a thousand times over and involved you in debt and ruin. Your confession only made me more determined to teach him a lesson. You've no idea how hard it was for me to restrain myself once I had disarmed him.'

The image his words had conjured up made a shiver pass down her spine.

'Please, Juliet, don't allow him to ruin your life for a second time.' He cupped her face between his hands and tilted it upwards. 'If you can look me in the eye and tell me I am mistaken and you don't care for me the least little bit, I will never trouble you again.'

She was lost in those eyes. She struggled to find the right words, not knowing what she wanted to say.

'Oh, Richard, if only you knew . . . '

Without warning, an arm slid around her, drawing her into the shade of the nearest apple tree and closer to his breast.

'I think I do know,' he whispered, just before his lips disappeared from her sight and pressed instead against hers, teasing them apart in a long, hungry kiss.

THE END

We do hope that you have enjoyed reading this large print book.

Did you know that all of our titles are available for purchase?

We publish a wide range of high quality large print books including:
Romances, Mysteries, Classics
General Fiction
Non Fiction and Westerns

Special interest titles available in large print are:
The Little Oxford Dictionary
Music Book, Song Book
Hymn Book, Service Book

Also available from us courtesy of Oxford University Press:
Young Readers' Dictionary
(large print edition)
Young Readers' Thesaurus
(large print edition)

For further information or a free brochure, please contact us at:
Ulverscroft Large Print Books Ltd.,
The Green, Bradgate Road, Anstey,
Leicester, LE7 7FU, England.
Tel: (00 44) **0116 236 4325**
Fax: (00 44) **0116 234 0205**

Other titles in the
Linford Romance Library:

DANGEROUS FLIRTATION

Liz Fielding

Rosalind thought she had her life all mapped out — a job she loved, a thoughtful, reliable fiance . . . what more could she want? How was she to know that a handsome stranger with laughing blue eyes and a roguish grin would burst into her life, kiss her to distraction and turn her world upside down? But there was more to Jack Drayton than met the eye. He offered romance, excitement, and passion — and challenged Rosalind to accept. Dared she?

ROMANTIC LEGACY

Joyce Johnson

Wedding plans in ruins, Briony Gordon immerses herself in her job as senior wine buyer at Lapwings Wine Merchants until a dramatic turn of events forces her to reconsider her future. A substantial legacy from her beloved Grandfather gives her the incentive to explore new possibilities. At Moonwarra winery in Western Australia, Briony finds feuding brothers quarrelling over the Winery's future — a future which gives her a wonderful business opportunity and where she finds true love . . .

CONFLICT OF THE HEART

Dorothy Taylor

A summer job, as live-in nanny, caring for seven-year-old Ellie seems like a dream for Karen Carmichael. But while Ellie proves a delight, her father, archaeologist Neil Oldson is hard to get to know. Karen puts his reserve down to pressure from the looming deadline on the nearby Roman site he is managing. But when valuable finds from the site are stolen, her growing feelings for him are thrown into doubt. Then Karen's life is put in danger.